“WHO IS
HE ASKED

“A cat. Your kitchen cat. The cat in your Tribeca restaurant.”

Dan Wu stared at me for a full thirty seconds without answering. It was a most peculiar look. I simply couldn’t fathom it, but it made me uncomfortable.

Then he asked, “You saw a cat in my restaurant?”

Was he pulling my leg? What was going on?

“Of course I saw a cat. A big red tabby. She was lying on one of the high shelves in the kitchen.”

“Was the cat looking at the moon?” he asked.

“No. The cat was looking down at the customers.”

Again there was a long silence. Was he serious about a cat looking at the moon?

Then he said, “What you saw, perhaps, was a dragon.”

“Please, I don’t have time to play with you. The cat—your kitchen cat—vanished the night of the shooting. What happened to her?”

“I know of no cat,” he said calmly.

“ENTERTAINING.”—*Booklist*

THE ALICE NESTLETON MYSTERIES BY LYDIA ADAMSON

☐ **A CAT IN THE MANGER**—***An Alice Nestleton Mystery.*** A beautiful sleuth finds that cat-sitting can be murder when she unwittingly steps into a deadly conspiracy. (167872—$3.99)

☐ **A CAT OF A DIFFERENT COLOR**—***An Alice Nestleton Mystery.*** A mystery cat takes a talented actress-turned-sleuth behind the scenes—for murder. (169557—$3.99)

☐ **A CAT IN WOLF'S CLOTHING**—***An Alice Nestleton Mystery.*** A cat, a mouse, and two corpses equal a menagerie of mystery. (170857—$3.99)

☐ **A CAT BY ANY OTHER NAME**—***An Alice Nestleton Mystery.*** The gorgeous gumshoe discovers a dead woman's dearest friends may well have been her most murderous enemies. . . . (172310—$3.99)

☐ **A CAT IN THE WINGS**—***An Alice Nestleton Mystery.*** When the murder of former ballet great Peter Dobrynin is pinned on Alice's close friend, Lucia, she is drawn into a dark and dangerous dance of deception as she snoops from the flop houses of New York to the elegant salons of wealthy art patrons for the real killer. (173368—$3.99)

Prices slightly higher in Canada.

A CAT IN A GLASS HOUSE

An Alice Nestleton Mystery

Lydia Adamson

A SIGNET BOOK

SIGNET
Published by the Penguin Group
Penguin Books USA Inc., 375 Hudson Street,
New York, New York 10014, U.S.A.
Penguin Books Ltd, 27 Wrights Lane,
London W8 5TZ, England
Penguin Books Australia Ltd, Ringwood,
Victoria, Australia
Penguin Books Canada Ltd, 10 Alcorn Avenue,
Toronto, Ontario, Canada M4V 3B2
Penguin Books (N.Z.) Ltd, 182–190 Wairau Road,
Auckland 10, New Zealand

Penguin Books Ltd, Registered Offices:
Harmondsworth, Middlesex, England

First published by Signet,
an imprint of Dutton Signet,
a division of Penguin Books USA Inc.

First Printing, November, 1993
10 9 8 7 6 5 4 3 2 1

Cover Art by Robert Crawford

The first chapter of this book previously appeared in *A Cat with a Fiddle.*

A CAT IN A GLASS HOUSE

1

I was holding big, beautiful Bushy straight out over the sofa, his luxurious Maine coon cat tail curling apprehensively beneath him, his big eyes staring at me suspiciously.

"Bushy, I think I'm going to become a movie star. How do you like *those* sardines?"

He squirmed out of my grasp and vaulted lightly to the carpet. Tail high, he strode away, his feelings ruffled. Well, Bushy is a skeptical cat. I had been skeptical myself, but something *was* happening.

Early that same morning I had received a phone call from my agent. She told me that a man named Brian Watts wanted to know if I was interested in doing a film. It was an Anglo-French production, to be shot in Malta. Yes, Malta, which I really couldn't place geographically beyond "somewhere in the Mediterranean." The director was French—Claude Braque, whom I had heard of. And the film was a political thriller about the IRA and British Intelligence. My character would be an evil, Garbo-esque CIA operative.

"Be gentle with him," my agent had said before hanging up. "The pay is very good." Judging by her tone, I was some kind of demented cat-sitter who couldn't be trusted in social interactions with movie people.

At noon, Brian Watts called. He was in Toronto, and would be arriving at Kennedy Airport around seven in the evening. Could he meet me at some restaurant downtown, around eight? Perhaps Dan Wu's, the new vegetarian Chinese restaurant in Tribeca? Of course, I said. Delighted, I said. And I surely was. Dan Wu's restaurant was a gastronomic jewel. So I had read. And I also knew from my reading that the price of a single meal there was equal to half my rent. But Brian Watts was picking up the check. Yes, I was delighted.

After all, Dan Wu was the author of *Five Flavors,* one of the best Chinese cookbooks ever written. I had purchased it three years ago, although I only got around to trying one recipe—ginger duck. Disaster . . .

So when Bushy was skeptical, it really didn't hurt my feelings. I was already thinking of the dinner ahead.

I spent a few hours daydreaming about what I would do with the enormous sums of money that would be coming to me for my rather belated screen debut . . . and about whether or not I would choose to appear at the Oscar ceremonies when I was nominated as Best Supporting Actress.

At six I had to make my dress decision. What does a forty-one-year-old stage actress cum cat-sitter wear to be courted, cinematically, in a posh Tribeca restaurant? Well, it *was* Tribeca, so I had to be a bit déclassé in order to be hip. And since it was obviously a big-role/big-money part, I also had to be a bit elegant. So I chose an ankle-length, vampish dress, rose-colored. Over it I wore a beat-up, short black denim jacket that had been given to me as a joke by my friend Basillio. No earrings. Long, yellow-gray hair loose.

I arrived at Dan Wu's on time, at eight. And Brian Watts was waiting for me in front of the restaurant. My heart sank when I saw him in the light reflected from the restaurant front. He was too old to be wearing the designer jeans he had on. He was too out of shape to be wearing the very hi-tech running shoes on his feet. And he was too agitated in manner to be wearing that very expensive and quite beautiful gray-on-gray silk sports jacket, which seemed to have been crumpled with care to exude that "laid-back" look.

Despite his British accent he was obviously very "Hollywood," and the moment we stepped through the door together he started a monologue, a kind of name-dropping babble about Bobby and Swifty and Larry. None of whom meant a thing to me, but all of whom, obviously, meant a lot to Mr. Watts.

The restaurant was breathtaking. The main dining room was circular. The walls were white and unadorned. The round tables were all glass. The chairs were glass, with black seat and back cushions. All the tableware was glass except for the chopsticks and other utensils, which were elegantly carved black wood.

The waitresses were beautiful young Chinese women, all dressed any way they wanted.

In the center of the main dining room was the kitchen—it seemed to have had sprung out of the floor, full-blown and totally open, in dazzling stainless steel. Wherever one sat in the room, one could see every step in the food preparation.

Four doors led out of the circle to the bathrooms, the cloakroom, and the place where the dirty dishes were cared for.

The multi-page, totally vegetarian menu sent me into a kind of rapture. I really wasn't familiar with a single one of the dishes. Oh, I recognized many of the ingredients, but not the dishes per se. For example, I knew both soy sauce and ginger, but I had absolutely no idea what "soy-marinated shredded ginger" would look or taste like. It was giddy reading. After all, I love Chinese food. The single most wonderful discovery I made about New York, when I first arrived in the city, was the ready availability of all kinds of Chinese food. For a farm girl, it was a revelation. And now, more than twenty years later, I was a farm girl again, because this was a whole new Chinese cuisine to me.

Brian Watts started to talk about a dinner he had had in a Chinese restaurant somewhere south of Los Angeles with Sue and Denny. It was obvious he thought I knew who they were. I didn't. I smiled at him and returned to the menu. In my business, no one ever gets to the point until dessert.

I read the menu as if it were a novel. Brian Watts kept up his monologue. From time to time I looked up from the menu and stared at him. He had a handsome face, just a bit bloated. His eyes kept roving over the room as he spoke, as if searching for friends. I felt neither affection nor enmity toward him. We were perfectly comfortable with each other. None of it was real, and neither of us minded.

Finally I made my selection. First I would have Sweet Peanut Soup with Strawberries. Then I would have Shredded Bean Curd with Golden Needles, Mushrooms, Wood Ears, and Eggs.

Just giving the order to the waitress was exciting. Of course, I had absolutely no idea what "Golden Needles" were.

Then Brian Watts, for the first time, looked at me long and hard and a trifle critically . . . and, for the first time, I realized that he was looking at me in that weird way "sophisticated" men often do with women they don't approve of.

"What you ordered," he noted, "is just a kind of vegetarian Mu Shou Rou." Since I didn't know what "Mu Shou Rou" was, there was nothing I could say.

I smiled. He started to talk again. I felt more friendly toward him. My eyes moved toward that stainless-steel island of a kitchen, where white-garbed geniuses were creating remarkable tastes. One saw pots and flames and woks and knives being manipulated, but heard few sounds.

Then I saw the cat. An enormous red tabby, napping like a rag doll on the ledge of one of the stainless-steel shelves, high up.

The only parts of tabby moving were the tail and one twitching paw. What a wonderful place to snooze, I thought. And what a beautiful kitchen cat!

Yes, Dan Wu's was a spectacular dining spot. No doubt about that.

Our waitress appeared and placed on the table a glass carafe of hot tea and two small glass cups.

Brian Watts expertly picked up the carafe by its long neck and started to pour tea into my cup. For a moment I panicked. Hadn't Brian Watts had a grandmother who warned him never, never, never to pour hot tea into a glass without first placing a spoon in the glass so that it doesn't shatter? He obviously hadn't. But it didn't matter. The glass did not break.

I sat back, relieved. Brian and I smiled at each other.

Then I looked back at the high kitchen shelves. Red Tabby had awakened and was gazing condescendingly at the customers, lazily counting the house. What a beautiful cat!

Suddenly my eyes filled with tears. I blinked them away. The red tabby had brought back to me a wonderful childhood memory: my grandmother, rocking herself to sleep on her chair with Henrietta on her lap. Grandma had "inside" cats and "outside" cats, barn cats and house cats—but she had only one lap cat: big old red tabby Henrietta.

I had an overwhelming desire to rush to the high shelf and grab Red Tabby. Then I would bring her back to the table and rock her in my lap . . . just like Grandma used to rock Henrietta. But I didn't move.

Red Tabby knew what I was thinking, though. I could see that. I could sense it.

I smiled once again at Brian Watts, to let him know I was back on his wavelength.

"You did some rep work in Montreal, didn't you?" he asked.

There was no doubt about it—he had a very handsome face. A bit like Terrence Stamp.

"Yes, I did. Some Shakespeare."

"Then we probably know the same people up there," he noted.

I didn't answer. At that moment, something very strange happened.

The restaurant became absolutely still. There hadn't been much noise, anyway, just the usual low hum and the sounds from the stainless-steel kitchen island. But even those minimal sounds ceased. I mean, the place went completely mute.

I looked at Brian Watts. He was staring past me, and his face had grown pale. I turned in my chair to follow his gaze.

Three young men were standing casually, side-by-side, about ten feet into the main room. They were Chinese. They were handsome and well dressed. They seemed very young, almost teenagers. Their jackets were much too large for them, and too long. They wore shirts and ties.

Each carried a small, ugly, blackish object in his hands, cradling the object gently as if it were a bird.

Then one of them detached himself from the group and walked to a wall. He removed a can of spray paint from his jacket pocket and began to draw a single large Chinese character in red paint on the brilliantly bare white wall.

The hostess came out of the stainless-steel kitchen, walking toward the graffiti artist. She walked slowly, obviously frightened and confused. She was speaking to him in Chinese, in a low voice.

The artist flung the spray can at her, striking her on the neck. The hostess staggered backward. Someone in the restaurant screamed.

Then the shooting started. Brian Watts threw himself to the floor. I did the same.

It wasn't like in the movies. The firing sounded somehow distant. Dull, staccato bass grunts. It was the results that brought the terror. The bullets chewed up walls and glass and seemed to splinter everything. I was so frightened that my fingernails bloodied my palms.

Then there was silence again. Slowly people began to get up and look around, but there was little to see because it was dark. The three young men had vanished. Brian Watts helped me up.

The lights had been shattered. Someone opened the doors that led out of the main dining area, so that light could filter in.

Ten feet away from our table lay our waitress, her right leg and right arm stretched out. Her long black hair, which had been tied up, now wreathed her face. Her hair was speckled with a pattern of blood. Her face had a look of absolute repose, but her eyes were wide open. She obviously was dead. I started to cry. I tried to get to her, but my limbs were no longer taking commands. Brian Watts was trying to light a cigarette. I began to shake. And then the strangest thought came into my head: *I will never, as long as I live, taste Sweet Peanut Soup with Strawberries.*

2

A dark-haired, childish-looking uniformed policewoman stood at our table. Her notebook was open. Other police officers stood by other tables, their notebooks open. A procession of police and medical people crisscrossed the shattered dining space. The body of the dead waitress had been removed. There was an enormous bloodstain on the floor.

"May I have your names and addresses?" she asked kindly, but with authority. Brian Watts gave her three different addresses: one in LA; one in London; and one in Toronto.

I saw the name on the tag over her left pocket: BRODT. Officer Brodt. She verified the time we had been seated for the dinner we never had, and the time we first saw the three gunmen. Then she asked us to recall whatever we remembered of the three young men.

Brian Watts perked up. His nervousness and pallor seemed to vanish. It was obvious he was going to use this tragedy as grist for future dinners, telling it and retelling it as a director would recount memories of a particularly difficult "shoot."

"They were Chinese," he said, "between the ages of nineteen and twenty-five. They wore their hair long, but not too long. Two of them carried their weapons in their right hands, and one in his left hand. They wore shirts and ties. One of the ties had a flower pattern. They wore suit jackets, but not matched to their pants. The jackets were fashionable about two years ago, during the brief Forties revival. The shooting started after the hostess was hit by the spray can."

Watts pointed to the wall, where the inscrutable Chinese character stared out over the carnage.

"I never heard them speak a word," he added.

Then Officer Brodt turned toward me, waiting for me to add what I could.

"They looked younger to me," I said. "About fifteen or sixteen." I was about to add that they looked as young as Officer Brodt, but caught myself at the last moment. It would have been impolite.

"Did you notice any distinguishing marks? Scars? Tattoos? Anything like that?" Officer Brodt asked.

We shook our heads.

"Did you see where they entered from?"

"No," Brian Watts replied. "I just looked up and there they were, standing right there." He pointed dramatically toward the center of the circular dining room. I could see the cinematic images forming in his head. Was it going to be a black-and-white film? I doubted it.

Then he did a strange thing. He poured himself some more tea, sipped it, and grimaced. "Ice-cold," he said.

Officer Brodt stared at him for a moment. Then she flipped her notebook closed, thanked us for our time, told us that we would be contacted at some future date, and moved to the next table of dazed diners.

"I suppose we can leave now," Brian Watts said, surveying the scene with an almost triumphant air, as if it were our wit that had enabled us to survive.

I didn't answer. Suddenly I felt very weak.

"And it's just not the time to talk about why we're here," he said, "so let me take you home in a cab. I'll be back in New York in a few weeks and we can get together then. There's no rush." He stared at the enormous bloodstain on the floor. There was still not enough light in the dining area, and the stain seemed oddly discolored.

Then the blood emptied from his face in a rush. "Was it our waitress who was killed?" he asked suddenly, in a whisper.

"Yes," I replied.

We sat there for a long while without saying anything. Then he stood up, helped me up, and escorted me out of the restaurant. He held my arm tightly, as if we two comrades had endured a great battle. I did not like that.

In the cab, I disliked his behavior even more. He kept asking me in an overly solicitous tone whether I was well; whether he could do anything for me; whether I wanted some aspirin or a drink. I kept saying 'No, thank you' again and again. Undoubtedly he was working me into his next dinner story. First it was impersonal—his lady friend who fell apart during the shooting. Then I could hear him describing me personally to his Hollywood friends:

Oh, you've never heard of Alice Nestleton? How odd! Quite an actress she is . . . something of a cult figure in Manhattan. Never achieved stardom, of course, but the critics love her. At least some of them do. And she has a reputation for eccentricity.

She's a cat-sitter in her spare time. Are you sure you've never heard of Alice Nestleton? A tall woman with blondish hair; long hair? The wrong side of forty, I would say, but well preserved.

Yes, I could hear all of that, in Hollywood/ British argot.

He actually kissed my hand when I left the cab. It was a long, wearisome climb up to my apartment. The shock of the shooting was still with me. Oh, I was no newcomer to the realm of murder. I had investigated murders, I had seen dead bodies. But I had never been in the center of it before, never been an eyewitness to such a violent and horrific murder. I had never been *there* . . . right *there* . . . as the bullets splintered the walls all around. My life had been too genteel to shake it off quickly.

Finally I reached my landing and let myself in, collapsing immediately on the sofa.

Sitting in the hallway, just visible by means of a bit of kitchen light (I always leave it on when I'm out for the evening), were my two cats—Bushy and Pancho. It was odd to see them sitting there so calmly, close together. They usually have nothing whatsoever to do with each other. And Pancho, poor dear stray that he was, rarely rests from his perpetual flight from imagined enemies. But there they were, sitting for their portrait.

"I'm back," I called out to them. "But whether or not I'm going to be a movie star has not been resolved."

Silence.

"In fact," I informed them further, "the dinner did not turn out as planned. The service was tragically interrupted."

Pancho vanished. Bushy went into the kitchen. I was alone.

I fell asleep on the sofa, sitting up, still in my black denim jacket. When I awoke, three hours later, it was past midnight. My mouth was dry. I walked slowly into my small kitchen to get some apple juice.

As I opened the refrigerator, I looked up to the top of the high cabinet to see if Pancho was there. The high places are where he loves to hide.

No, Pancho was not there. But it was at that precise moment—as I stared upward, holding the bottle of apple juice in my hand—that I remembered the cat in the restaurant.

What had happened to that wonderful red tabby who was snoozing on top of the stainless-steel shelf?

I walked swiftly back into the living room, still holding the unopened bottle of apple juice.

Very agitated, I began to pace. Why hadn't I looked for the cat after the shooting? Why had I forgotten about the cat? After all, it wasn't just *any* old cat. Was it?

It was the great-great-great-great grand-niece of Grandmother's beloved Henrietta. It was a real red tabby lap cat, high up on the stainless-steel shelves. It was a cat that had brought back very beautiful memories. It was somehow, in some way, Grandma's cat. Up there. High up on the shelves.

I tried to recall the exact sequence of events. It had to be only seconds after I saw the cat that the shooting had started. Well, not seconds. Maybe two minutes. And after the shooting—what had I seen? Nothing. At least, nothing of the cat. But I had not looked for it. I had forgotten all about the poor Kitchen Cat.

It was all too much to bear. I collapsed once again onto the sofa, cradling the bottle of apple juice in my arms. The thing to do was run a bath, but all I could do was contemplate it.

3

Late the following morning, around eleven, while I was dully dusting my living room furniture, the door buzzer began to ring. I ignored it at first, figuring it was a mistake. But it kept on ringing. Who could it be?

My friend Basillio was in Bucks County, Penn sylvania, interviewing for a stage manager's job at a thriving summer playhouse. He had given up his set-designing career for the moment, and just wanted some kind of theater work.

The ringing persisted, so I executed the standard Manhattan door-buzzing procedure. I pushed my button, allowing the outside door to open. Then I opened my apartment door, left it ajar for a hasty retreat, and positioned myself at the top of the landing so that I could see who was climbing the stairs at least one landing before mine.

I heard heavy steps and male voices. I became frightened. Who was it? Criminals? Or had I ordered something to be delivered and forgotten all about it in the aftershock of the shooting?

Then I heard a familiar voice call out, "Alice Nestleton! Isn't it about time you moved down to a more accessible floor?"

Into view came the florid face of Detective Rothwax, my old friend from RETRO, the NYPD special unit where I had once, so very briefly and unhappily, worked as a consultant. Since my dismissal from RETRO I had often asked for Rothwax's help, but it was always I who had initiated contact. I was astonished that he was paying me a social call, unannounced. Behind him was another man, who didn't seem to be minding the stairs as much.

Rothwax grinned when he reached my landing. "You better have some coffee ready."

Once inside my apartment he turned to his companion and quipped, "Be careful, Sonny, she has two attack cats, and they show no mercy."

Rothwax sat down heavily on the sofa. "Alice, this is Detective Emerson Hoving. We call him Sonny. He works with me at RETRO."

I shook hands with the younger man. He was thin, dark, intense, handsome. Unlike Rothwax, who wore a suit and tie, Sonny wore a washed-out turtleneck and one of those hiker's vests. His hair was very black, and brushed back with a vengeance. After we shook hands he stepped back away from me, quickly, delicately, like an athlete or a dancer.

"Well, you may be wondering what the hell I'm doing here," Rothwax said, stretching his arms out along the back of the sofa, "and I'm going to tell you that it is one of the weirdest coincidences in the history of RETRO."

I had no idea what he was talking about, and my face obviously betrayed my puzzlement.

"It's simple, Alice, but it's really strange. Sonny and I were going over the witness list the crime-scene cops compiled on the Chinese restaurant shooting . . . and there it was, as plain as the nose on my face: none other than Alice Nestleton. So

I figured I'd come over and see what you were doing in such a posh restaurant at that particular time."

"I was there to eat," I said. "But tell me what RETRO has to do with a restaurant shooting."

Detective Rothwax grinned. "I see you haven't been keeping track of us, Alice. Judy Mizener was fired a couple of months ago. RETRO was no longer cost-effective. So we changed course. No more looking back into unsolved major cases. RETRO now deals with organized crime; we're part of a city/state/federal push. But not old-fashioned LCN cases."

He was using that police language again. "What does LCN mean?"

"La Cosa Nostra. You know, Mafia. No, RETRO is starting to deal with the new mobs in town. The Russians and the Chinese, the Jamaicans and the Dominicans."

The younger detective had begun to walk around my living room. He seemed to be inspecting my possessions.

"I still don't understand. What did the shooting last night have to do with organized crime?"

"Dan Wu is dirty," Rothwax replied.

Rothwax called out to his partner, who was now staring out my window, "Sonny, you tell her. It's your case."

Detective Hoving seemed to ignore Rothwax. He didn't say a word. Rothwax chuckled and said, "Sonny is sometimes a bit shy. Well, Alice, let me put it this way. We think Dan Wu is involved in a few—how shall we say—criminal enterprises. And we think the shooting last night wasn't just one of those cases of trigger-happy Chinese or Vietnamese youth gangs shooting up fancy restaurants for protection money."

Detective Hoving then spoke for the first time. "Do you have a napkin?"

"A what?" I asked. "A napkin."

His voice had not the slightest trace of a New York accent. He sounded, in fact, a little like someone who had once received voice training. He articulated each syllable.

"In the kitchen," I replied.

He walked quickly into the kitchen, obtained a paper napkin, came back to the living room, and crouched right beside me—holding the napkin on one knee while drawing on it with a pencil.

"Do you remember this?" he asked, holding up the napkin. On it was what looked like a Chinese character. It was the same character one of the gunmen had spray-painted on the wall of the restaurant.

"Is it the symbol of some kind of secret society?" I asked.

He laughed out loud and crumpled the napkin. "No. It's the Chinese character for soup."

"Soup? That's hard to believe."

"Believe it."

"But why would someone spray-paint it on a restaurant wall?"

"Maybe the gunmen were making a joke. Or maybe they really didn't like the soup there," he replied.

Rothwax said: "Listen to Sonny, Alice. He's the only Mandarin-speaking cop in RETRO. And his mother is Chinese."

So that's it, I thought. A Eurasian. No wonder he seems ill at ease with everyone and everything—even though he's a very attractive young man. He's an outsider.

"What about some coffee, Alice? If I remember, you make very good instant coffee."

I turned and started toward the kitchen. Then I stopped and slowly turned back. It was important that I take care of first things first.

"Did either of you hear anything about the kitchen cat?" I asked.

"You mean in the restaurant?" Sonny Hoving queried.

"Yes. There was a big red tabby in Dan Wu's kitchen. I was watching him when—"

Peals of laughter burst from Rothwax, cutting me short. He stood up, almost drunk with mirth, and grabbed the younger detective by the shoulder. "My God, Sonny, I forgot to warn you about her! She has this crazy thing with cats. She sees cats lurking around every corner. In RETRO we used to call her Cat Woman."

Sonny Hoving stared at me, confused. Then he said, simply, "I saw no cat in the restaurant. No one told us about any cat."

I walked into the kitchen and made three cups of instant coffee. Then I placed several slices of seven-grain bread and a small jar of apple butter onto a plate and brought everything into the living room, setting it on the long table.

Rothwax made a face when he saw the seven-grain bread. "I know you prefer powdered donuts with fake grape jam," I said with a wicked grin, "but I'm all out."

Bushy joined us. We all sat down together and drank our coffee, primly.

When we had finished, Rothwax opened his jacket expansively and said in an officious tone,

"And now, Alice Nestleton, we want to know exactly what you saw last night. Everything you can remember. From the moment you walked into the restaurant until the moment you left."

"And I really thought this was a social call," I replied.

But then I told them what I remembered of the evening, every scrap I could remember: conversations, impressions, the menu, everything.

When I had finished, Rothwax nodded appreciatively and asked, "Was the woman who was killed your waitress?"

How odd! Brian Watts had asked me exactly the same question.

"Yes. Do you know her name?"

Rothwax stared at Detective Hoving, waiting for him to respond. When the younger man didn't, Rothwax flipped out his notebook and read: "Nancy Han. Age nineteen. Lived with mother downtown. Student at the Fashion Institute of Technology. Clean as a whistle." He flipped the book closed. "In fact, I don't think those kids meant to shoot anyone. They had a lot of firepower, but they seemed to be firing high on purpose."

I caught Detective Hoving staring at me, and suddenly I felt very uncomfortable. I stood up and started to clear the cups away. My guests mistook it as a sign that I felt they should leave—and they did so, quickly.

4

Two hours after detectives Rothwax and Hoving had left my apartment, I began to get angry. Really angry. But my anger didn't spring from Rothwax's sardonic contempt for my concern over a kitchen cat. No. It was the whole style of the typical NYPD investigation. They did it their way. They *always* did it their way.

A beautiful young woman was dead. Shot to death in the most terrible manner. And Rothwax and his colleagues had decided, for their own reasons, that her death was a tragic error, that the gunmen had killed her by mistake. That the gunmen were in the restaurant for other reasons, reasons that RETRO had decided were plausible—some kind of organized crime connection.

RETRO had decided that the lovely student at New York's prestigious Fashion Institute of Technology had been an innocent victim.

That probably was the case. But they hadn't asked Nancy Han's mother. Had they? They required cartoons, not complex dramas. That was their childish nature.

Calm down, Alice, I kept telling myself. Maybe they have asked Nancy Han's mother. Maybe they just didn't tell me. Maybe they were exploring more complex plots than they'd had time to tell me about.

Clearly, my anger was misplaced. But something else was going on in my head. Maybe the horror of what had happened was just beginning to hit me. Maybe it was the fact that the red tabby had brought back such intense memories of Henrietta, my grandmother's red tabby lap cat, her pride and joy.

Then all kinds of crazy motifs started to run through my head.

Why had *my* waitress been murdered? Why not some other waitress? Why was it the young woman who had taken *my* order? And why was this red tabby an *exact* replica of my grandmother's Henrietta?

Oh, it was the kind of feeling I had experienced many times in the past—but only in relation to the theater. Many times I had found myself with a part in a play that I just couldn't grasp. The character eluded me. No matter how many times I read the script, no matter how many times I consulted with the writer or the director—I just couldn't grasp it.

I tried to nap. I tried to read. I tried to clean. I tried to brush Bushy. All to no avail.

By two in the afternoon I knew one thing for sure: I had to speak to Nancy Han's mother. Maybe to question her. Maybe just to give her my condolences. Maybe to assure her that her child had died suddenly, without pain. I laughed at my own cruel arrogance. Without pain? The woman's daughter had been snuffed out in the most painful manner possible—randomly. If not randomly, then selected for execution.

But I *had* to speak to Nancy Han's mother.

I opened the Manhattan telephone book. Rothwax had said Nancy Han lived with her mother, *downtown.*

There were eleven parties by the name of Han who lived south of 14th Street. I started to dial the first on the list, then stopped. What would I say? Quickly, I constructed a script and recited it to the dead phone. "Hello. My name is Lucia Allen. I'm a classmate of Nancy's at FIT. I just heard the terrible news. May I please speak with Mrs. Han?"

Then I dialed. The first two Hans didn't answer. The next three hung up.

On the sixth call a man answered and listened to my monologue politely. Then he said, "Thank you for your call, Miss Allen. Unfortunately, Nancy's mother has gone to stay with a relative. I will relay your message of condolence to her. Many of your fellow students have already called."

And that was that. We both hung up the phone. As futile and as silly as my call had been, it made me feel much better. I lay down on the living room sofa and fell fast asleep.

Twenty minutes later I jumped up—frightened, sweating, chilled.

What a horrible dream it had been! An afternoon nightmare. Young Asian men were spraying the restaurant with gunfire, trying to kill the red tabby cat. Only this time it truly was my grandmother's cat, Henrietta herself.

For a moment I was totally disoriented. I thought I was back in Dan Wu's restaurant. But then I saw Bushy and I knew where I was.

I started toward the kitchen and stopped in my tracks. I remembered more of the dream. The hostess had saved Henrietta.

The thought came to me that I was in shock, that I was suffering some kind of delayed trauma, that I was in the throes of post-traumatic-stress syndrome.

Then I remembered what I had forgotten to tell not only the young policewoman who had interviewed me at the scene of the crime but also Detective Rothwax when he'd come up to my apartment.

That the hostess had bravely interceded with the gunmen. That she had approached the gunman with the spray can and spoken to him in Chinese.

How could I have forgotten that? She had been so brave. Everyone else in the restaurant was petrified, only she had acted.

I began to pace again. It was obvious to me that she was a superior woman, and if she was a superior woman she would love cats, and if she loved cats she would have a special relationship with the red tabby. Yes, for sure. She would know that the cat was well. Or if the cat was hurt, she would know where it was and whether it was being treated. And she might know a lot more . . . maybe even about Nancy Han.

I rummaged frantically around my apartment until I had come up with thirty dollars in assorted bills. Then I threw on a denim jacket and ran down the steps, hailing the first cab I saw.

Ten minutes later I was on Franklin Street, in Tribeca, across the street from Dan Wu's restaurant. I paid the fare and ran across the street to find her.

Of course, the restaurant was closed. I deflated like a pierced balloon.

What a fool I was! Had I really believed the restaurant would open up again right after that tragedy? How could I have believed that? I stepped back. What should I do? I didn't know her name. Rothwax would know, but it would be a hassle to get it out of him. He would start that "Cat Woman" nonsense all over again.

There was a small gourmet shop two doors from the restaurant. I walked inside and asked the young man behind the counter if he knew the name of the hostess of Dan Wu's restaurant. He looked at me very suspiciously. He would tell me nothing.

I walked out. There was a commercial stationery store near the corner, just about to close. Perhaps the restaurant had an account with them. An encore of the same scene: suspicion and silence. Did they think I was a cop? Or an insurance adjuster? What?

Then I walked into a small cleaning store. The proprietor was Asian. His wife was in the back. I told him that it was very important for me to contact the hostess at Dan Wu's.

The man's eyes flooded with tears. "So terrible. It is so terrible what has happened. Poor Anna Li. A lovely woman. She brings her clothes in here every Thursday morning, and I deliver them to her on Saturday."

"At the restaurant?" I asked.

"No, no," he blurted out. "At her home. On Bowery and Broome. In the blue building on the corner."

I started to walk out. He called after me, suddenly worried at what his grief had let slip. "Wait! Who are you? Why do you want Anna Li?"

But another cab was beckoning to me.

* * *

The three-story building at the corner of Broome and Bowery was rundown on the outside, but the inside hallway was spotlessly clean. Anna Li's name was listed next to 2C. I pressed the buzzer and kept my finger on it. I was buzzed through, and climbed the one landing to the second floor.

I could see that there were security cameras on either end of the landing. That was obviously why I had been buzzed in so perfunctorily. Then I rang the buzzer on the side of 2C's door.

A weird static seemed to come from the knob, and then the door swung open as if on an electronic signal.

I found myself staring at a beautiful Chinese woman dressed in a pair of green silk pajamas, buttoned all the way up to the neck. She was shoeless. At first I didn't recognize her, for her hair hung loose. But then I realized that this was, indeed, Anna Li, the hostess. In the restaurant she had worn her hair up.

She stared at me.

"My name is Alice Nestleton," I declared anxiously. "I was in the restaurant during the shooting. Nancy Han was my waitress."

She didn't respond. Something was very strange.

Then I realized that there was a glass door between us. She hadn't heard a word I'd said.

I gestured that she should open the glass door so that I could talk to her.

She wouldn't.

I started to pantomime a cat to the best of my ability, to show her that all I wanted was information on the red tabby.

Slowly, the outside door began to close. I

stepped out of the way quickly and it slammed shut.

I rang again. She didn't respond. I rang yet again. Silence.

I walked slowly down the stairs, onto Broome Street, and took a cab home.

I crawled into my bed and snuggled with Bushy. This episode, I said to myself, is over and done with. This case—to use a RETRO phrase—is no longer in my jurisdiction.

5

By the third day after the shooting, the shock had diminished. I returned to a normal existence. I listened to my agent tell me that the movie part was, in her opinion, secure, and that Brian Watts would indeed return to New York shortly to offer it. I listened to my cat-sitting clients tell me exactly what their friends really needed in the way of care. I listened to Basillio on the phone telling me that I should withstand the lure of any "loft forays into The Theater of the Absurd" until he got back to New York. His suggestion was, as usual, cryptic.

At the stroke of noon, on the fourth day after the shooting, the phone rang. I was cleaning the two large windows in the living room that look down on East 26th Street; the only two windows in my apartment that I can look out of. It was the last gasp of my spring housecleaning, a rural phenomenon I'm still addicted to as an anodyne to crushing guilt. For my grandmother in Minnesota, only death and spring cleaning had any religious significance.

I picked up the phone. A male voice said, "Millie."

I replied, "You have the wrong number."

"No!" the voice replied, aggressively. "I mean the cat's name is Millie."

"Who are you?" I asked, now very confused.

"This is Sonny Hoving. The name of the cat you saw in the restaurant is Millie."

"Is she okay?" I asked quickly, anxiously, not bothering to apologize for not having recognized his voice.

"I don't really know. I believe so. No one has seen her since the shooting. But if she had been hurt we would have found her. She's probably hiding. The shooting probably frightened her so much she went into hiding. There are a lot of cellars and storerooms in the restaurant."

"It was very kind of you to call," I said. There was a long pause, and I hadn't the slightest idea what else to say. I was too astonished that he had called at all . . . had really made an effort to find out about the kitchen cat.

"How is everything going?" I finally managed to inquire.

Silence.

"I mean, with the restaurant shooting."

"Nothing new," he replied.

Another uncomfortable pause. Finally he said, "I'm going to be in your neighborhood this afternoon. How about a drink with me?"

His offer came out of the blue, and it confused me. Then I remembered that I had a cat-sitting chore to take care of that afternoon. Saved from hurting his feelings, I explained my situation.

"I like cats. I'll go with you."

For some reason, without thinking, I just laughed into the phone and said, "Why not?"

The moment I hung up I felt that nagging, low-level anxiety attack coming on, the one that tells me I've made a mistake.

Sonny Hoving met me on time in front of the massive high-rise building on First Avenue and 31st Street, just across from NYU hospital. The woman I was working for was named Ginny Marley. I don't know what she did for a living, but she tended to take six-day weekends. She needed someone to make sure her cat, Hannibal, was happy while she was away.

The studio apartment she lived in was almost devoid of furniture. It had, however, a magnificent oriental rug. Hannibal was in his usual spot, on the windowsill, gazing out over First Avenue. He was a stubby middle-aged black shorthair, with white on his front legs and on his crown. And we didn't seem to bother him at all.

Sonny Hoving followed me about as I prepared Hannibal's food, cleaned the litter box, watered the three plants. It was odd; I felt perfectly at ease with him there. Perfectly at ease and unrushed as he watched me work. He didn't say a word, but seemed to have a genuine curiosity about what a cat-sitter does.

When my chores were done, I sat down on the windowsill, about five feet away from Hannibal.

"Now what?" Sonny Hoving asked. I smiled at him. The detective was wearing a different color turtleneck—a very washed-out green—from the one I had seen him in previously, and the same hiker's vest. But this time he wore beat-up running shoes and jeans, and where the jeans met the shoes I could spot a bulge. That was where he carried his weapon, I realized, in an ankle holster. He looked very, very young.

"Now I have to talk to Hannibal. His mistress told me that Hannibal likes to be talked to."

"About what?"

"The weather, I guess." So I started a short dialogue with Hannibal, nothing cute or anything, just a matter-of-fact discussion about the vagaries of spring sunlight and the traffic outside and what Hannibal had been watching lately as he gazed down onto First Avenue.

And then we left.

Once outside the building, Sonny Hoving said, "Listen, I asked you to join me for a drink, but I really don't drink. Could we have coffee instead?"

"Fine."

We walked to a small Italian-style coffee shop on 34th Street between Second and Third Avenues. It had lovely tables with pink tablecloths and served forty-one different kinds of coffees and teas.

We sat across from each other and ordered espressos.

When the coffee had been placed in front of us, Sonny Hoving went through an elaborate ritual of turning the cup, measuring out the sugar, and stirring it. I could see he was not at ease. But then neither was I.

Finally he sipped his espresso, put the cup down, and said, "You're very beautiful."

"So are you," I said quickly, without thinking, and believe it or not I started to blush, or at least flush.

Then we both laughed.

"Rothwax tells me you're a famous actress," he said.

"Hardly famous," I replied. "If I was, would I charge for cat-sitting?"

"And he tells me that you're a fine criminal investigator when you want to be."

"That's kind of him," I noted.

"And he tells me that once in a while you become a crazed cat woman."

I smiled at him. He stared down into his espresso, picked up his spoon, and began to tap it lightly against his cup. Something very strange was going on between us, but I didn't know what. I had a powerful urge to pick up my small spoon and also tink it against the side of my cup. But I didn't.

"I want to tell you about myself," he said suddenly, almost urgently.

I smiled. I had heard those kinds of words and that kind of desperation before. From that young man, Bruce Chessler, who had fallen in love with me when I was teaching a class at The New School; the one who had left a strange white cat on my doorstep just before he was murdered. Was that what was going on here? Another young man baring his soul to an older woman he desired? Looking for the woman who would both console him and drive him wild? Or was it something less mundane?

"Go ahead."

He shook his head from side to side. "No. If I start talking, I'll never stop."

"We could order more espresso," I said gently, trying to be helpful.

"The question is . . . why do I want so badly to talk to you about myself?"

"I don't know."

He played with his spoon again, then changed the subject. "You don't think Dan Wu is a bad guy . . . do you?"

"I don't know the gentleman. All I know is what I've heard about him. And I read his cookbook. I can't form a judgment from that."

He dropped the subject. The silence came again. We stared into our cups.

Then he said, "You know, I'm not that much younger than you."

I didn't reply. He leaned forward and spread both hands out on the table, palms-up. "Look," he said, "my hands are shaking."

Then he pulled his hands away from the table, onto his lap. Out of sight. I had a sudden urge to hold one of the vanished hands.

"Listen," he said, "did you ever hear of the Jade Society?"

"No."

"It's a charitable association made up mostly of wealthy Chinese-Americans. It benefits new Asian immigrants. I'm a very lowly member, and one of the few Eurasians in it. And one of the few with a yearly income of less than a quarter million. But I attend the annual dinner, and it's being held this Sunday at the Waldorf. Would you come with me to it? Good food, good drink, and boring speeches."

"I don't know."

"Please."

"Okay. . . . Why not? What do I wear?"

"Anything you want. Anything." He smiled very broadly. His face seemed to have lit up. "By the way, Dan Wu will be there. He's a major benefactor of the Jade Society."

I had accepted his invitation because he was so nice. But the moment he mentioned that Dan Wu would be attending the dinner, I became intrigued. I wanted to tell Sonny about my strange adventure with Dan Wu's hostess, but I held back, figuring it would not be prudent. After all, this handsome young man did work for Rothwax.

"What time do you want me to be ready?"

"I can pick you up around six."

"Fine. Just ring the downstairs buzzer and I'll come down."

He leaned forward toward me. "I want very much to see you again, Alice. Very much."

Before I could reply he began to scribble on a napkin with a ballpoint pen. At least, I thought he was scribbling. Then he pushed the napkin toward me. I could see he had drawn a Chinese character.

"Well, I know it's not the character for soup," I quipped.

"No, it's the character for devil."

I felt uneasy. "Why draw such a character?" I asked. "Am I a devil?"

"No, no! I drew it because of the old saying—you know, 'The devil's got your tongue.' I drew it because I can't seem to tell you what I feel."

"There will be time for that," I said.

6

I did something very strange the evening of the Jade Society dinner. Actually, I did several strange things. For one, I dressed a full hour before Sonny Hoving was supposed to pick me up. Now, that is something I just *never* do. But I did it, and sat waiting on my living room sofa for the buzzer to ring.

Second, I dressed very strangely: a shortish black evening dress, with bare shoulders and tiny straps. And I put my hair up. At first I thought nothing of my selection, even though I always wear long dresses and my hair long, straight down with a vengeance.

As I waited, the embarrassing truth assailed me: I was trying to dress younger. Poor me! Poor Alice Nestleton! Was this only a flirtation? Why was I acting so peculiarly? He was so much younger than I, almost a child. No! That was ridiculous. But he obviously did have a childish crush on me. His behavior in the coffee shop had made that very clear.

YOUNG EURASIAN COP, SMITTEN WITH OLDER, WORLD-WEARY ACTRESS. Would it make the gossip columns?

I sat on the sofa and glared at Bushy so that he wouldn't amble over and deposit cat hairs on my dress. No, that just wouldn't do. What was going on? I was at least ten years older than Sonny, probably more. And I did have a particular friend—if one could characterize Tony Basillio as that.

I did like Detective Hoving very much. He was feline, and so few straight men are feline. He was nimble and quick and secretive and beautiful. Beautiful? What was going on in my head? Beware the Jabberwock, Alice. Beware.

It was a long, introspective hour. When the buzzer rang I walked regally downstairs and into the waiting taxi. Sonny was wearing a dark suit and a lovely spring topcoat. The knot of his tie was too large, but I took it as a sort of sartorial joke.

"You look beautiful," he said. I didn't reply. We sat next to each other, primly, barely touching. It was as if we both recognized that there was danger. That we would have to be careful.

The taxi pulled up in front of the Waldorf and a uniformed man opened the door. We waltzed through the lobby as if it were perfectly natural for us to be there and entered a large room through two elaborately carved doors.

Along one wall was a banner on which large Chinese characters had been printed. "Self-help, charity, and justice," Sonny translated. Then he added: "The motto of the Jade Society."

The room was already filled with Chinese people dressed to kill. There were two enormous buffet tables set at right angles to each other. Beneath the wall banner was the raised dais. In the center of the room were dozens of tables and chairs.

I breathed a sigh of relief. There were no reservation cards on the tables, no assigned places to sit, like at a wedding. One just took one's plate from the buffet tables and brought it to an empty table.

We sat down at a table and sipped our drinks.

Sonny had ginger ale. I had white wine. Then Sonny left and brought back two plates filled with savory goodies. I asked what the dishes were.

He pointed to the first plate. "Stir-fried zucchini in Fu-Yung sauce." Then he pointed at the second plate. "Stir-fried asparagus with garlic."

I had taken only one mouthful of zucchini when Sonny whispered, "Well, well. Look what we have here. The devil himself."

I followed his gaze to a nearby table, at which three people sat.

"That gentleman on the left is Dan Wu," Sonny said.

He was a distinguished-looking gentleman of about sixty with brushed-backed snow-white hair. He wore a Mao suit, a fashion long obsolete even among Chinese.

"Do you recognize the woman next to him?" Sonny whispered.

The back of my neck stiffened. She had her hair up again, and this time she was wearing a very chic, conservative business suit. But it was Anna Li . . . the hostess . . . the woman who had stared silently at me from behind the glass door.

"No," I lied.

Sonny grinned. "That's Anna Li, the hostess at his restaurant."

I vowed silently to confront her—gently, politely, without vindictiveness.

"And the one on the right is Jack Pallister," Sonny explained, "Wu's business manager. Every Chinese hustler needs an Anglo front man, don't they?"

Pallister looked to be in his forties; a florid man wearing an ill-fitting tux and an equally ill-fitting cummerbund. He wore a string tie and looked drunk.

"Let's greet our friends," Sonny said sarcastically.

"Do you know them?" I asked, a bit frightened.

"Dan Wu knows me," he replied. "He knows I know he's dirty."

Sonny escorted me to their table and introduced me to them all.

I really didn't know what to say, so I told Dan Wu that I loved his cookbook. The great chef beamed.

Then Jack Pallister asked, "Are you *the* Alice Nestleton?"

Everyone looked at me strangely. I looked at the man blankly.

"The actress. Are you Alice Nestleton, the actress?"

I nodded.

He laughed. "I knew it! Don't you remember me? Many years ago, at that funny theater on West Fourth Street. The one shaped like a skating rink. We were bit players together. It was a crazy production of *Saint Joan*, set in Vietnam."

I didn't even remember the production. He stood up, grabbed me by the arm, and started to walk away with me, saying pointedly and only half-humorously, "Us theater people have to keep our distance from the philistines." I slipped out of his grasp and walked back to Sonny's side. The man was tipsy. And a tipsy old actor is very bad news.

"You never know who you'll meet," Sonny remarked as he escorted me back to our table. The speeches started. They were dreadfully boring, and most of the guests seemed to ignore the speakers completely. The chatter among the guests never ceased, just grew muted, and people continued to move about freely.

Sonny said, "I have to shake a few hands. It's an old Taoist custom." He kissed me on the back of my neck and left. It was done so casually and so quickly that I wasn't even surprised. But why had he kissed me like that? Was it a mere social gesture, springing from too much ginger in his ginger ale? Or was it arrogantly proprietary? He didn't own me. Or was it just childish exuberance? Or did he think I would sleep with him after the dinner because I had put my hair up and worn a foolish dress?

And thus I clothe my naked villainy. The line popped into my head. Where was it from? Shakespeare no doubt, but which play, and was I in it?

I spotted Sonny standing three tables away, talking to a very handsome, beautifully attired young Chinese couple. The woman's hair seemed to be down to her ankles. Sonny was leaning over and smiling, but his eyes were on me. They were so intense I had to look away, flustered.

Then I saw the hostess, Anna Li, alone near one of the buffet tables. She was staring at the speaker but didn't seem to be focusing; she seemed lost in thought.

I left the table and walked over to her. "Hello again." She looked at me but didn't answer. I smiled kindly. "Could you tell me if Millie is okay?" I asked.

She looked at me again, blankly. "Millie," I repeated. "The big red tabby in your kitchen. I didn't see her after the shooting. And I'm worried."

Without saying a word, without looking at me again, Anna Li walked away from me. Dumbfounded, I watched her return to the table where Dan Wu and Jack Pallister were seated.

It was incredibly rude of her. I didn't know what to think. Was the hostess still in shock from the shooting and the death of the waitress? Was she deranged? Deaf? Didn't she care about Millie? Or was Millie dead, and Anna Li too pained to speak of it? If not dead, perhaps grievously hurt.

"They go on and on," a voice whispered into my ear.

I wheeled around. It was Sonny. "But you will admit," he continued, "it's much less stuffy than most charity bashes. Did you notice that no one listens to the speakers and the speakers don't seem to care at all?"

"Chinese people always have good sense," I replied.

"Yes they do," Sonny said. "But not Eurasians." He grasped my hand, hard. "Let's get out of here. Let's go for a walk. Let's make believe this is a real date."

I smiled. "Where will we walk to?"

"Uptown. Downtown. What does it matter?"

I looked across the room to the table where the Wu entourage was seated. What a strange trio they were. They sat very close to one another but didn't speak. They all stared at the current speaker but seemed not to be hearing a word. The hostess, Anna Li, who was seated between the great chef and the ex-actor turned business manager Jack Pallister, had her hands folded on the table as if she had just been chastised by the teacher.

"Well?" Sonny asked.

"Well what?"

"A walk."

"Sure," I said. It was a mistake.

7

It was a lovely night for a walk. We headed south on Lexington, past Grand Central Station, and didn't say a word until we were south of 30th Street, that stretch of Lexington that has all the Indian spice stores.

Then Sonny took my hand and started to talk—a nonstop autobiographical torrent. About how his father worked for the Motor Vehicles Bureau on Centre Street and used to wander through Chinatown on his lunch hour. How he'd met his wife in a Chinatown store that sold greeting cards. How they'd fallen in love and married. How they were still together in California, where they'd moved after they'd retired. How he'd grown up in Queens, gone to the Pratt Institute to study engineering, then had dropped out and taken the exam for the NYPD. How he loved being a cop, but had no friends among the cops. How he'd taken a trip to northern China three years ago, to see the village where his mother's mother had been born.

I was listening, but my eyes were focused on his hand. Why were we holding hands? It seemed that I hadn't held hands with anyone for years. The grip itself was strange. He wasn't holding my hand strongly. Rather, our hands just nestled together, as if they had been formed that way in some other life and then had just sought each other out. I caught myself—these speculations were getting mystical. Never get mystical about a man.

He stopped talking suddenly, the moment we reached Gramercy Park. "I'm babbling, aren't I? Really babbling. I'll tell you why. Because I want you to think highly of me. Yes, isn't it pathetic? I'm trying to impress you with how sensitive I am . . . how well balanced . . . analytical . . . admirable. You know what I mean?"

"Yes, Sonny, I know what you mean." He squeezed my hand hard and we skirted the western edge of the park and headed toward 14th Street. From there we walked to University Place.

"How about stopping in the Cedar Tavern for a minute?"

I nodded my assent. It had been years since I was in that bar. When I first came to New York it had been de rigueur to go there; after all, it was the legendary center of the art and poetry world. It was where the crazy downtown geniuses drank themselves into a deeper oblivion.

The bar was not crowded. The enormous wooden breakfront was still there. The lighting was still poor. The service was still friendly. Sonny and I took a seat near the door. He ordered his ginger ale. I ordered a glass of red wine.

"Did you find the Jade Society dinner too painful?" he asked.

"Not at all. I enjoyed it. And I enjoyed very much meeting Dan Wu." Even in the bar's murky light I could see his face cloud over at the mention of Wu's name. Then I told him how Anna Li had totally ignored my question about the health of the kitchen cat, Millie.

Sonny didn't think it very odd. He said that all people associated with Dan Wu, in whatever capacity, were very closemouthed.

"But this is just about the well-being of a harmless cat," I remonstrated.

Hunched over his ginger ale, he didn't answer. We sat there for the longest time together, in silence, listening to the buzz at the bar and the background music. It was pleasant, very pleasant, even though the wine was terrible.

Then, suddenly, he picked up the glass of ginger ale and pressed it against his forehead to feel the cold. It was a common enough gesture, but for some reason I felt an incredible surge of tenderness for him immediately after he made it. I reached over and began to massage the back of his neck gently. His neck was tight, like a piece of steel. The touch of my hand made him flinch for a moment—but then he relaxed.

When I pulled my hand away he moved very close to me. "You know . . . I have never met anyone like you, Alice. You are beautiful and you are smart and you are different and you listen and you understand. And there hasn't been a moment in the day or night since I first met you with Rothwax that I haven't thought of you."

"That's unfortunate," I replied, laughing, trying to defuse his intensity, if only for a moment.

"I want us to be together, Alice."

"Yes. I understand that."

"I want us to be lovers. To be together. To see each other all the time. To make love and take walks and sit in bars. To cat-sit together. And if you want I'll even goddamn *act* with you. I want all that very much, Alice."

"Yes, I know you do."

"But tell me what you think. Do you want that, too? Am I crazy in thinking you do?"

"No, not crazy."

Everything was moving fast. Too fast.

"Let's get out of here," he said suddenly, urgently.

"Where are we going?"

"I'll show you."

We left the bar and crossed the street. "I live there," he said, pointing to a large loft building on 12th Street, east of University. We climbed slowly up three steep flights of stairs. He was so nervous he couldn't open his lock, fumbling and almost breaking the key off. Then we were inside. It was a small apartment with a very low box-mattress bed. A television set and cassette player were next to it on the floor. There were two large chairs at either end of the room, and on the freshly painted white walls hung several watercolors. A cool breeze crossed the room from an open window. I could see he had no real kitchen, only a walk-in alcove with stove, small refrigerator, and old-fashioned one-basin sink.

I stared at the mattress and then at him. I wanted very much to touch him. I wanted very much for him to touch me. I was no longer thinking about processes or consequences or why or how all this had happened.

He kissed the palms of my hands and said, "I am very happy now."

We undressed quickly, without another word, and lay down together. What happened next was quite wonderful, special. Either I had forgotten all about sex-in-love or had really never experienced it, despite my forty-one years. It was simple and uncomplicated and there was no thought involved. We both knew what to do. We both knew what would give and elicit pleasure. We both wanted the other to be, if you will pardon the banal words, both ecstatic and exalted.

I could not get enough of him. He could not get enough of me. It was gentle and violent. It was swift and slow.

And then it was over. We lay side by side, drenched in sweat, and the breeze blowing in from the window was slightly chilling.

Sonny fell asleep immediately, like a cat, one arm beneath his head and the other sprawled out over my breasts.

I could not sleep. I just lay there, stunned. I knew what had happened. I had fallen in love. Hopelessly, in fact. I had fallen passionately in love with a total stranger. It was like a bad imitation of that Trevor Howard movie whose title I can never remember.

The noise from a private sanitation truck on the street below exploded into the small room. Sonny stirred, but did not wake. That noise, however, brought me back to reality. What would I tell Tony Basillio? What *could* I tell him?

8

I waited for Sonny's call . . . that was all I waited for. And it came thirty-six hours after that wonderful night in his apartment. He was on duty. He couldn't call before. He was working. I understood. Could I meet him at the Cedar Tavern on University Place in about an hour? Of course. I would have met him there in twelve minutes. I was in love, and I was forty-one years old. The mix is potent.

As for Basillio, I had not called him. Or written him. But everything had been suspended. Acting. Cat-sitting. Memories of Brian Watts, and Millie, and the dead young woman on the restaurant floor. The promise of love dissolves everything. Doesn't it?

There was a faint echo resonating in my head. Like Poe's Raven. Only it kept saying quietly: *Wrong, Alice. Wrong, Alice. This is all wrong.* Or sometimes it said: *A trap, Alice. A trap. A young man can only wring your heart out.* But I ignored the echo.

It was late afternoon. The place was empty. Sonny and I sat in a booth. He ordered a ginger ale and a rare hamburger. I ordered a glass of white wine and a pasta salad.

Neither of us could eat or drink what was

brought to us. I stared at his arms, exposed because he had pulled up the sleeves of his faded turtleneck. What strong, lovely arms he had—thin but muscled. Beneath the table both our legs were pressed together; we were like adolescents.

We started to laugh. It was absurd sitting there contemplating food we didn't want, trying to make words we couldn't summon. We knew where we wanted to be. We left the food and drinks and walked out.

We started to make love as we climbed the stairs to Sonny's apartment. Ten seconds after we'd passed through the door, we were on the bed.

It was a kind of frenzy. We began to pull our clothes off.

And then, suddenly, I stopped and stood up. The echo in my head had become a clanging bell: *This is all wrong. Wrong! Wrong! Stupid!* And yes, pathetic. I had to stop. I had to think.

"What's the matter?"

For a moment all I could say was, "Everything's the matter, Sonny."

He stared at me dumbly.

I tried to get my thoughts together. All I really knew was that I didn't want the affair to continue like this—jumping in and out of bed. I didn't want a series of one-night stands. Something was missing. Something was awry, and the intensity of the sex was just filling the gap . . . and in a way, frightening me.

All I could say was, "I need some time, Sonny."

"Time for what?"

"This has all happened so fast, Sonny. I'm not interested in random sex anymore. I'm too old for games."

"Random sex?" He repeated the phrase as a question, with a quiet fury. And then said, "Maybe you wanted flowers first. Maybe you wanted me to court you like a princess. Is that it, Alice? I wasn't gallant enough for your theatrical tastes." His voice had turned bitter.

All kinds of replies came into my head. I wanted to tell him about Basillio. I wanted to tell him that I was frightened. I wanted to tell him about my grandmother. I wanted to tell him that my feeling for him was very strong; that I had really loved the sex; that I enjoyed every moment I spent with him.

"I need more time," was what I repeated.

He got off the bed and started to pace. Why had this whole thing erupted so suddenly? An hour ago I wasn't even thinking of ending the relationship. All I was thinking about was getting into bed with him. Maybe it was just plain common sense. I am not a modern woman.

He stopped pacing and said: "Okay, okay. We'll play it your way for a while. I can handle celibacy. You're the first woman I've slept with in a long time."

Then he brought two glasses of water. One for him and one for me.

"Besides," he said as he handed me the glass, "I have a worse problem than you."

"What?" I asked, happy that the subject was being changed.

"RETRO," he replied.

"RETRO?"

He was very close to me, half-naked, one foot on the bed and one foot on the floor. He kept staring at the glass, as if it were important for me to drink. So I drank.

"Yeah, RETRO. You worked there. You know how it sucks."

"Well, I was just a consultant there. They hired me on a whim. But you're a police officer. It's home."

"Home?" He shook his head sadly and brought his foot off the floor so that he was totally on the bed beside me.

"Do you know what my good buddies in RETRO say about me when I'm out of earshot?" He asked.

"No idea at all."

"They say the only reason I made detective is because I can speak Chinese and the Department is desperate for people like me."

He plucked the glass out of my hand and rolled it foolishly along the floor like a bowling ball. I didn't like the way things were going. He seemed to be fading from me, to be thinking only about RETRO. I wanted him with *me*, beside *me*, thinking of *me*.

"And I'll tell you something else," he said in an accusatory tone. "Your friend Rothwax doesn't think much of me either."

"He's not really my friend," I lied mildly.

"Your friend thinks that I'm way out of line with Dan Wu. Rothwax wouldn't give you a dime for what I got on him. Even after the restaurant shooting. In fact, I'm about the only guy in RETRO who really believes that Dan Wu is dirty." He got off the bed and began to pace. "Do *you* believe it?" He finally asked.

"You asked me that question before, Sonny. I told you I don't know what to believe. But in my heart, I guess I just can't believe that a gentle, dedicated, literate chef like Dan Wu could be a criminal. I mean . . . is nothing sacred?" I meant my reply to be somewhat humorous, but Sonny didn't get my intent at all.

He stared at me for a long time, as if he couldn't believe what he had heard.

Then he strode to a small chest in the corner of the apartment, pulled out a file folder, rummaged around in it, and extracted what appeared to be a photo.

He brought the item back to me and flipped it down onto the bedspread. "Take a look at *that*!" he barked.

I found myself staring at a photo of two men engaged in a conversation on a Manhattan street. Both were wearing overcoats. It was not a normal kind of photo. It seemed to have been taken by a telephoto lens, with neither of the men knowing they were being shot. It had that odd anonymous quality to it—like news photos. And the print was grainy.

"Do you know who that is?" Sonny asked, sarcastically.

"It looks like Dan Wu."

"Damn sure does. The Literate Chef himself, Dan Wu. Now look at the other man closely. Do you know who he is"

"No."

"His name is Felix Lapidus. We were conducting a surveillance of him when this photo was taken. Lapidus is international sewerage. He brings together buyers and sellers from around the world. Narcotics. Stolen gems. Weapons. Anything."

Sonny tapped the photo near Lapidus's grizzled face. "Felix was murdered at JFK airport four days after this photo was taken. We brought Dan Wu in. He denied even meeting Lapidus. We showed him the photo. Wu claimed he had forgotten . . . that the man had simply stopped him on the street for directions. Look at the photo again, Alice. Does it seem to you they're talking about the subway?"

I looked carefully at the photo. Dan Wu had his head bowed, as if he were listening to something very important. Felix Lapidus had his hand on Wu's shoulder and seemed to be whispering something near his ear. No, it didn't look like a chance encounter. But who could tell? It was a surveillance photo, frozen in time.

Then Sonny was back on the bed beside me, his hand running along the side of my face. His eyes were burning, weird. "I'm going to get him, Alice. Do you believe me?"

"Yes, Sonny, I believe you," I replied.

9

We were spending a chaste day together, Sonny and I, in keeping with our new relationship. We had met for breakfast in the morning on 23rd Street, then taken a long walk uptown to the Central Park Zoo. I felt that I had done the right thing. I felt that I needed more time. I felt unpressured now.

We sat in the dark coolness of the penguin house watching the penguins being fed. Two young women had entered the pen, which was masterfully designed to mimic the penguins' habitat, including a fast-running and deep body of water in front of the "ice." One woman checked the number on each penguin against her tally on the clipboard as the other patiently hand-fed each penguin two fish. One from pail A and one from pail B. It was obvious that one of the pails contained fish stuffed with evil-smelling vitamins and supplements, because the penguins had to be persuaded to take the second fish after gleefully swallowing the first.

It was so peaceful there. I leaned my head on Sonny's shoulder. Everything about this affair was odd, I realized, and sooner or later I would have to break it off completely or go to bed with him again.

It was odd that, although we seemed to bask in each other's presence, we rarely spoke to each other. At least we didn't attempt significant conversation, the kind one usually indulges in when one falls in love.

The only real conversations we had were about Dan Wu and the restaurant shootings. Or rather, they were about Sonny's frustration over the lack of progress in the case and his inability to prove that Dan Wu was "dirty."

I had never told him about my brief, manic fling at investigating this case—the telephone calls, and the wild cab rides to locate and speak to Nancy Han's mother and Anna Li. All futile. And I never told him about my mild obsession with Millie and her uncanny resemblance to Henrietta. I couldn't bear the thought of Sonny laughing at me in a Rothwax/RETRO mode.

Everything about that horrible night in Dan Wu's restaurant still festered inside me. It was there, close to the surface. I was happy that Sonny had showed me the surveillance photos, but perplexed that he had done so the moment I had put a halt to the sex.

Yes, everything about this affair had become odd. What were we to each other? What would we become?

"Do you know, Alice, that if I had to be reincarnated in some future life I would like to come back as a penguin?" Sonny paused. Then added: "Or as a killer whale."

"Spoken like a true cop," I said, laughing. "Either end of the predator-prey chain."

"I didn't know killer whales eat penguins."

"They surely do, Sonny."

He thought for a while. "No, it's not the predator-prey link that intrigues me. It's the cold. I like cold places. Maybe it's because my great-great-great-great grandmother fell in love with a Mongol."

"I would prefer to be reincarnated as a feral Maine coon cat . . . or, if that's not possible, a solitary bumblebee."

"And spend your days going from flower to flower?"

"Exactly."

Suddenly a raft of penguins began to dive into the water, one after the other. Once they were beneath the water we could see them through the glass, swimming at great speed, like purposeful, tuxedoed torpedos.

A group of school kids wandered into the exhibit, pressed their faces against the glass, and stared at the submerged penguins, who seemed to respond to their gaze with a series of breathtaking underwater acrobatics. Then they all clambered out and stood around, looking confused.

"Are you hungry?" Sonny asked.

"Not really."

"Do you want to go to a movie?"

"I don't think so."

"We could walk back downtown . . ."

"Sure," I agreed. But we didn't move. We watched as the two women finished their feeding chores.

After the feeders had left the exhibit I started to stand, but pressure from Sonny's hand kept me from rising.

"I found out something very strange," he said by way of explanation.

"About what?"

"Dan Wu has decided to close down his Tribeca restaurant."

"But why?"

"He says he's closing it because of the death of the waitress. He says he's too filled with sadness at what happened to continue."

"And you don't believe him?"

"Not for a minute."

"When is he closing it?"

"Today. Tomorrow. Or maybe yesterday."

"Why do you think he's closing it?" I asked.

"It has to be something very threatening to him. That restaurant was a gold mine."

"Then it had to be the shooting. Was it a warning to close up?"

"I don't think so. Something else. Some kind of payoff or payback. Some kind of crazy deal. But guys like Dan Wu don't get scared off, and they don't give a damn if one of their waitresses gets blown away."

"My, you're hard on him," I noted.

"Not half as hard as he is on me!" Sonny said passionately. He spoke those words with such feeling that for the first time I understood his almost manic determination to get Dan Wu. It seemed to go to the very core of him as a Eurasian cop.

"Any word on Millie?" I asked.

"No, nothing."

"What about those young men who blew the restaurant apart?"

"Nothing. We had all the waiters and kitchen help study mug shots of every Asian under thirty who has been arrested in the past seven hundred years. Nothing. It might simply be that those kids don't have any record at all. Or it might be that Dan Wu's staff have learned to keep their lips sealed."

Sonny leaned forward and placed his head in his hands. He seemed distraught. I ran my hand through his hair. It pained me to see these sudden flights into what could only be despair. And I had no real idea what caused them. Was it because I had withdrawn sexually? Was it because he couldn't prove that Dan Wu was "dirty"? Was it the strain of being a half-Chinese cop in a decidedly occidental NYPD?

If it was the latter, I couldn't help him. If it was his failure with Dan Wu, I was not yet ready to help him, and besides, I knew in my heart that he would not appreciate my interference. If it was that other thing . . . my stepping back from his bed . . . well, it had to be that way for now. But only for now.

And oh, I so much wanted to help him. If I didn't love Sonny Hoving, it was the closest thing to love I had experienced in a long time. If only he hadn't been associated with my old nemesis, RETRO.

A very sobering and bizarre thought popped into my head: What if I had fallen in love with Sonny Hoving because he *was* associated with RETRO . . . and because he just might be the only one who could clear up what had happened to a lovely red cat who happened to be a replica of my grandmother's Henrietta, the cat who brought back to me the most intense, bittersweet memories of what childhood is all about?

Suddenly Sonny straightened up. "Let's go see the polar bears," he said. "They're always good for a laugh."

Are they? I wondered. But I followed him anyway.

10

The phone woke me. Who could be calling at six-thirty in the morning? Bushy's one open eye stared at me sleepily from the adjoining pillow. He wasn't about to answer it. I did, groggily.

"I love to wake you up, Swede. I just love it." My longtime companion was having his fun. His voice, however, pushed me into a kind of numbness. I knew I would have to tell him about Sonny.

"Are you with me, Swede?"

"How is it there, Tony?" I asked gently.

"Of course they love me. They desperately need my brilliant dramaturgical mind. They want to hire me as stage manager for a three-play summer repertoire, at a rate of eleven dollars a week and all the splinters I can pull out."

"How's the weather, Tony?" I was fighting for time.

"There is no weather here. And besides, Swede, you don't give a damn whether I'm hot or cold." He laughed at his own words.

So I did it then in a measured voice, as if it were a majestic exit line: "Tony . . . I have met someone."

There was silence at the other end.

"I met someone," I continued, "and it—"

"Shut up, Swede!" he said harshly into the phone. Then I heard him breathe deeply. "You don't have to tell me anything, Swede. So don't."

"But, Tony, I—"

"Shut up, Swede. The way I figure it is that we're each entitled to two affairs a year."

"I love him, Tony."

There was no answer on the other end. "Tony! Did you hear me?" No answer. "Tony!" I literally screamed his name into the phone.

Then the phone clicked and I heard a dial tone. He had hung up.

I grabbed a pillow and flung it angrily across the room. Bushy panicked, leaped off the bed, and ran from the room, almost running over Pancho who was, of course, zooming into the room.

What a disaster! Why had I told him? Why hadn't I waited?

Even more reprehensible: Why hadn't I told him that I had stopped sleeping with Sonny? Why had I led him to believe that I was in the throes of a continuing erotic love affair?

Given the macho culture Basillio came from, he was awash with sexual jealousy, no matter how hard he tried to suppress it. He would be tormented. What a cruel woman I was turning out to be! Or if not cruel, just damned unthinking.

Miserable, I walked into the kitchen and boiled water for instant coffee. Then I took the cup into the living room and sipped the hot, sweet black brew while staring out onto the street from my window.

My hand holding the cup was trembling. The conversation with Basillio had truly been terrible. I didn't want to hurt him—and I had. I just wanted to let him know that nothing that had transpired between Sonny Hoving and me would diminish what I'd had with him. What a fool I was!

Pancho leaped onto a chair, then onto the windowsill, then along the top of the bookcase, and finally zoomed out. But he had knocked over a small postcard of a cow I always keep propped up on the empty edge of the bookcase—a Minnesota dairy cow, I might add.

I walked wearily over and righted the card, then smiled when my eye caught a familiar book spine. I pulled it out and stared at the reproduction of a famous twelfth-century Sung dynasty painting that had been reproduced on the cover of the book. It depicted a banquet attended by Chinese scholars all attired in their official robes. An elegant but hungry group of gentlemen. Holding *Five Flavors* by Dan Wu reminded me of the very sad news that Sonny had told me: Dan Wu was closing his Tribeca restaurant.

Even though I had been inside the restaurant only once . . . even though my meal had been interrupted by a tragic murder . . . even though I hadn't tasted a single dish—I was profoundly saddened over the closing. The restaurant, everything about it, had been special.

I took the book to the sofa and sat down. It was like holding an old friend. What has always made *Five Flavors* so wonderful isn't the recipes, as good as they are. It's the way Dan Wu ushers the reader into the inner sanctum of Chinese cuisine and discourses on its . . . philosophical foundation, if one can use that pompous phrase to describe the preparation of food.

Five Flavors had taught me things I simply did not know before. Such as the basic difference between *fan* foods—grain, rice, etc.— and *ts'ai* foods—meat, vegetables, etc.—and how they can be mixed but never merged. And the importance of the basic flavors of Chinese cuisine: bitter, sour, hot, salty, and sweet.

I held the small book in my hand and felt its lightness. It was really a very small book, clothbound, only a hundred and fifty-six pages, with large type, lovely paper, and chock-full of exquisite reproductions of Chinese paintings and prints, including many along the margins of each page.

I placed my coffee cup down on the small end table near the sofa and nostalgically began to flip through the pages.

Passing something familiar, I flipped back to find it. It was elusive, so I began to flip more slowly until I had found it.

The large Chinese character intrigued me and made me uneasy. Then I realized it was the same character that had been spray-painted on the restaurant wall; the character that Sonny had translated as "soup."

Indeed it was—the familiar character was the frontispiece for Dan Wu's chapter on soups.

I started to read the chapter, which, like all the others, consisted of a long introduction and then the specific recipes. I remembered it well. He talks about how soup is so important in Chinese cuisine, because only in soup can one truly create a perfect harmony between all the flavors and all the different kinds of foods.

I stopped reading for a moment, perplexed. The first time I had read the book, Dan Wu was not yet known as a vegetarian chef—his recipes weren't vegetarian, and he had yet to open his vegetarian restaurant. The vegetarian development, in fact, was a bit confusing and contradictory. After all, in his book he seems to insist that the genius of Chinese cooking lies in the fact that it restricts the use of virtually nothing—least of all meat.

I started to reread the book. At the end of the soup introduction, Dan Wu writes: "Every soup recipe that does not come out as it should is my fault. Every successful soup can be attributed to the wisdom of Ch'in Shih."

I stopped reading again. Odd, I didn't recall from my first reading of the chapter three years ago any mention of a "Ch'in Shih." I had no idea who that could be.

I closed *Five Flavors* and walked back to the bookcase to reshelve it. The sadness of the restaurant closing and Tony's response to my confession —disparate as these two events were—seemed to merge and infiltrate the slim volume. I felt that I was placing a body in a burial vault.

The moment *Five Flavors* was back on the shelf, I thought of Millie, the kitchen cat.

I stood there dumbly, staring at the spine of the book.

How could I have been so stupid?

Why hadn't I realized, when Sonny told me the news, that the closing of the restaurant meant disaster for Millie, if she was still alive and hiding in the restaurant. Now she would be sealed in—abandoned in a space she could not escape from.

To hell with worrying about Cat Woman jokes! To hell with Sonny's sensibilities! To hell with *everyone's* sensibilities. I ran to the phone and dialed Sonny's number.

11

It's amazing what an NYPD detective shield and ID card can do. A huge, menacing private security guard, pacing in front of the closed-down Dan Wu's in Tribeca, just waved us happily past him. Inside, the bright morning sun filtering through the windows revealed that a thin layer of dust had already been laid down.

I felt very strange suddenly, as if I were in a darkened theater rather than a shuttered Chinese restaurant. And the young man with me seemed to have been transformed into a dancer or a player, dressed in court costume. I had the funny feeling that the two of us should hold hands and bow elegantly to the audience. I remembered a snatch of a poem: "Love bade me enter. . . ." Was that why I was there? Had I really found the fellow player I had always sought after? The Lunt to my Fontanne? The Cronyn to my Tandy? The Burton to my Taylor? Was this baby-faced cop my leading man?

"The search begins," Sonny said, jarring me out of my reverie. As I looked about me, I saw that we stood in the once elegant dining room. The restaurant had been closed only for a few days, but it was a graphic example of how quickly elegance decays.

"Thank you for bringing me here," I said.

His hand caressed my face. "At this point in time," he said quietly, "I would do anything for you." I kissed him.

Then I whispered into his ear, "Brute beauty and valor and act."

"What?"

I laughed. "It's a line from a play I did, many years ago. The words are lifted from a Hopkins poem in which he is describing a falcon rising on a brisk morning wind. So, Sonny Hoving, sometimes when I look at you I think of that line. Brute beauty and valor and act."

"You're inflating me," he replied. Then he added slyly, "It's your way of telling me that I shouldn't be insulted you've decided to stop sleeping with me."

I didn't argue with him. *Where was Millie?*

Through the dining room we walked. The freestanding stainless-steel kitchen was grotesque in the gloom.

"That's where I saw Millie first," I said, pointing high up. "She was resting there, watching. A splendid, fat red tabby . . . beautiful and huge and groomed. Contented . . . Oh yes . . . she looked very happy. But also mischievous. Yes, I saw that in her also. A sense of the absurd. As if she were contemplating some little trick or two."

As we circled the kitchen, I went into my "Here, kitty, Heeeeere, kitty," routine.

Sonny stared at me incredulously as I progressed from words to caterwauling to unknown languages to groans that seemed to exude from my stomach.

All in vain. No response in the main dining room. We walked through one of the swinging doors and past the cloakroom. We checked the bathrooms and then took the stairs down, flicking light switches on as we descended.

The basement was massive. Bins filled with dishes and utensils and steamer baskets and supplies of all kinds lined the walls.

We looked in each and every bin for some sign of Millie: hair, droppings, even mouse skeletons in case she was hunting to survive.

No sign at all.

I opened a can of cat food and left it on the floor right in front of one of the bins, hoping the odor would draw out a still frightened but famished Millie.

Then we continued our search. The enormous refrigerators had been turned off and locked. We checked the vents and the overhead pipes and every conceivable hiding place. No Millie.

"Let's try the storeroom," Sonny said, taking me by the hand and leading me into the deep room through a wide-open door.

Stacked against the walls, almost halfway up to the ceiling, were crates of dried foods—primarily mushrooms and ginger root.

"Heeeeere kitty, kitty, kitty! Come out, come out, wherever you are, Millie!"

No sign. No sound. No sight.

"Look at this," Sonny said, tapping one of the crates.

Stenciled on the food crate was the name BANDA-ACEH.

"What does it mean?" I asked.

"It's the name of a port city in Sumatra, from where the crates are shipped." He studied the name for long time, seemingly intrigued by it. "Isn't it amazing," he finally said, "how Chinese food has spread all over the globe, on every continent. It's probably the only global food." He stared at me as if for confirmation, which wasn't forthcoming. "Except of course," he noted, "for Big Macs."

We searched for another fifteen minutes and then gave up, leaving the opened can of cat food just in case. But Millie was not in the restaurant. I was sure of it.

We walked uptown together, slowly, wandering through the spring crowds in Washington Square Park. I pointed to an empty bench near the chess tables. We sat down.

I was beginning to feel a sense of dread. Oh, not for myself or him—but for Millie.

It now seemed to me indisputable that Millie had been taken from the restaurant by the three gunmen. That she had, in fact, been kidnapped. At some point in their reign of terror, one of the gunmen had taken her. There was no question about it in my mind. A frightened, hiding cat would have left some kind of trace in the restaurant. If Millie had been in the restaurant after the shooting, I would have found something. No. She left with the gunmen.

But how could I tell that to the man sitting beside me? He had already been warned by Rothwax that I had crazy cat-woman tendencies; that I tended to read feline troubles into the most innocuous of cases.

No, I couldn't tell him Millie had been taken by force, against her will. But it was another goad to get into the Dan Wu case—to help Sonny and Millie at the same time.

"Can I ask you something, Sonny?"

"As long as it's not personal," he quipped.

"It's about the Dan Wu case."

"Ask away."

"Well, when I went to that dinner with you I watched the Wu entourage very carefully. Dan Wu's two companions seemed to be acting strangely. I was wondering why you didn't do any intensive background checks on them."

"What makes you think we didn't?" he replied testily.

"You didn't say anything about them to me."

"I don't tell you everything. Besides, Anna Li and Jack Pallister are just two of Wu's flunkies."

"How can you be sure they're flunkies?"

Clearly angry, he stood up. "Is the bench okay?" he asked, changing the subject and keeping his temper.

"It's fine, Sonny."

He stared at me for a long time, then sat down beside me again. "What are you up to, Alice? What are you angling for?"

"Well, I don't think I can be of any help when it comes to Anna Li."

"Damn straight you can't. Chinese people tell white investigators exactly what they want to hear."

"But Jack Pallister is another matter. He used to be in the theater. I can find out a lot about him, information the RETRO computer won't have."

"What's the matter, Alice? You got tired of the sex with me, so now you want to do some police work with me?"

"The sex was fine," I said gently.

He looked at me suspiciously, his lovely eyes glittering in the afternoon gloom. He seemed to be teetering on the edge of fury. Then he said, cavalierly, "Hell, Alice, do what you want to do. It can't hurt."

12

Why would anyone kidnap a kitchen cat? Millie was a handsome tabby, but not all that handsome. She was probably smart, but not all that smart. And moreover, those three young killers in the long jackets didn't seem like cat lovers. Still, it *was* possible they had staged the whole shooting just to take Millie. The thought was wild . . . dazzling.

I emerged from my walking reverie and looked up. The sign over the store read MATTRESSES. And beneath it was a smaller sign that read BEDDING OF ALL KINDS. I stared into the front window. It was a narrow, deep store with all kinds of bunk beds, mattresses, futons, hammocks, and other kinds of bedding and accessories lining the walls.

For two days I had been calling theater friends from the past for information on Jack Pallister. Most of my acquaintances didn't remember the man at all.

A few remembered him very vaguely as a "downtown" actor in the late Sixties and early Seventies with a reputation for eccentricities of various kinds. Quite par for the course.

One remembered him as a bit player in an "uptown" production of *Henry IV.*

Another person seemed to recall that Pallister

once gave a masterful performance in a coffee-shop production of Beckett's *Endgame.*

And then, happily, the name Renee Locke was mentioned, and it was hinted that Renee and Jack had been lovers. I contacted her, now a prim middle-aged woman who was executive director of a charitable fund that dispensed money for diverse health projects.

She didn't want to talk about her theatrical past. She didn't want to talk about Jack Pallister. She found all my questions distasteful. To get rid of me, she said that I should talk to a man named Nicholas Yagoda, who had been Jack's partner in a comedy team.

Comedy? Yes, Renee Locke affirmed. When he couldn't make it as an actor, Jack decided to become a comedian. Pallister and Yagoda were a team. Like Nichols and May. The problem was, Renee noted, they weren't funny.

But that was how I happened to be standing in front of a bedding store on West 14th Street, managed and owned by one Nicholas Yagoda.

Yagoda had survived his theatrical traumas well. He was a nattily dressed man of about fifty; short, fit, tanned, with styled hair. He looked like a low-keyed but very prosperous game show host.

"Can I help you with something?" he asked casually, one arm draped over a folded mattress bed on wheels.

"I'm from Citibank," I lied brazenly. He looked me over, first with simple curiosity, then with male lust. I continued. "Jack Pallister has applied for a rather large loan from our bank, and he's given you as a reference."

"Are you serious?" he asked. His face became

so threatening that I involuntarily stepped back, away from him.

"Quite serious," I replied, regaining my cool.

"I can't believe the sheer, unmitigated gall of that bastard!" Yagoda exclaimed. He made a half turn with his body, as if only the mattress on wheels could comprehend the absurdity of my inquiry.

Then he slammed his hand hard against the folded mattress frame. "Listen to me, lady, whoever you are! The only thing I want to hear about Jack Pallister is that he croaked! Then I can celebrate. The man is a two-timing, double-crossing, sleazy sonofabitch. He'll steal you blind!"

It was such a violent verbal response that I could only say, somewhat plaintively, "But you were his partner."

"Right. We did a comedy routine together. In nightclubs. He double-crossed me with agents, managers, and owners. He lied about the money. He lied about the bookings. Jack Pallister leaves oil stains everywhere he sits."

"Maybe it was just a misunderstanding."

He laughed uproariously at my comment. "You have a sense of humor, lady. You can't be a banker. Listen! Everyone who knew Jack Pallister for more than eight minutes knew that he was no good. No good! It took about eight minutes before he figured out a way to screw you. And screw you he did. Oh, he always did. Yes, he surely did."

Yagoda was beginning to talk fast—so fast he ran out of breath. He stopped, recovered, and began again.

"It took about eight minutes before he screwed you, but only about eight seconds before he went into his Chinese shtick. He likes people to think he's spiritual. He used to talk acupuncture and Chinese herbal medicine and all kinds of Taoist and Buddhist and god-knows-what other kinds of razzle-dazzle. That was just before he picked your pocket."

Suddenly his anger collapsed. He just went silent and shook his head and waved me away. I wanted to ask him if he meant that Pallister picked pockets literally, or just metaphorically. I wanted to ask if Pallister actually practiced acupuncture and herbal medicine or just talked about it. I wanted to ask a whole lot of things. But it was obvious that Mr. Yagoda was not going to say anymore.

I thanked him and left the store.

Never before had I dug up such revealing information on an individual so early in an investigation. If Jack Pallister was as bad as Yagoda said he was—even half as bad—then, for one thing, Dan Wu must have known what he was getting into when he took him on as business manager. Therefore Dan Wu *was* "dirty"—just as Sonny had said he was. And if Jack Pallister was as sleazy as Yagoda said he was, and if he took orders from Dan Wu, which he probably did, there was a very good chance that Pallister knew what the shooting was about . . . and what had happened to Millie. His fascination with things Chinese made the whole situation murky, but I had the intuitive feeling that it implicated him even further.

I breathed deeply, back out on the street. I was high—on a roll. I fed a quarter into a street phone. It didn't work. I lost the quarter. I fed another into its companion phone and reached Sonny.

He was in a hurry, just leaving his apartment.

He had to get downtown. I begged for five minutes.

"Meet me downstairs and you can walk me to the subway at Astor Place," he said.

I hung up the phone and walked quickly toward University and 12th Street. He was already pacing in front of his building when I arrived.

He grabbed my arm and we headed toward the subway.

"You in some kind of trouble?" he asked.

"No trouble," I replied. Then I told him what I had learned about Jack Pallister. He listened. He didn't say anything. We were only a block from the subway.

"Did you hear what I said, Sonny?"

"Sure. Good work. Some interesting facts."

"Well, don't you think you ought to put some kind of surveillance on Jack Pallister?"

"I don't think that's necessary."

"But, Sonny, he's probably at the center of all the nonsense." I bit my lip at the vulgarity of my own words. A dead young waitress was not "nonsense." Nor—for me, at least—was a kidnapped tabby.

"I doubt it. Look, I have to go."

"You're being hardheaded, Sonny."

His eyes flashed anger. "Don't call me stupid, Alice."

"I *didn't* call you stupid. I called you hardheaded."

"You meant stupid."

"Okay," I said, growing angry myself. "I meant stupid."

Then he yelled at me right in the middle of the street, said I was butting in where I didn't belong.

I turned and walked away from him as fast as I

could. Then he stopped yelling. He called out to me in a pleading voice, "Wait!"

I ran back to him. He put his arms around me. "I'm sorry, Alice. God, I'm sorry." We held each other. He kissed me. He whispered: "I don't want to fight with you, Alice. I don't ever want to fight with you." Then he walked down into the subway.

I stood there for a long time. I knew that to preserve harmony I and I alone would have to conduct the surveillance of Mr. Jack Pallister, lover of Asian mysteries and, perhaps, kitchen cats.

13

My concession to the science of surveillance was to wear a large straw hat with a red-white-and-blue streamer. Thus disguised, I arrived at Jack Pallister's domicile at seven-ten in the morning—alone, determined, secretive.

Pallister lived in a very beat-up building on 58th Street and Ninth Avenue. It seemed to me, at first, an odd place for him to live now, until I realized it must have been the apartment he had lived in as an aspiring actor. In those days, all starving actors and actresses worked way downtown, if they worked at all, and lived uptown, usually in or on the fringes of Hell's Kitchen. Uptown, then, meant anything north of 23rd Street.

Perhaps Jack Pallister still lived in that crumbling edifice because he had a sentimental streak. Or perhaps he was frugal. Or maybe it was the simple fact that Dan Wu didn't pay him the kind of money one would think commensurate with his exalted title: Business Manager, Dan Wu Enterprises.

Pallister emerged at five past eight. He wore a handsome denim shirt with a black tie, and a pullover sweater against the nonexistent spring chill. All actors are careful when it comes to chill.

His face was still florid, as it had been when he was tipsy at the Waldorf, but more fleshy. His thinning sandy hair was brushed back. He looked jovial. He looked focused. He walked briskly in spite of his paunch, which the cummerbund at the Jade Society dinner had done a superb job of hiding.

I followed happily, my straw hat pulled rakishly low over my eyes. After all, if he had recognized me at the banquet when he was high, he surely would recognize me on the street, even from the half-block distance I kept between us.

He continued walking south on Ninth Avenue. When we passed the Port Authority Bus Terminal I began to wonder if this stroll of his was really going nowhere, if it was just some kind of circular walking workout.

He finally stopped at a standup counter on Ninth Avenue and 35th Street and had a muffin and coffee. Then he continued south down the avenue.

I was wearing sponge-soled walking shoes, but still my feet were beginning to ache from the strain of the surveillance.

Then Pallister abruptly turned east on 23rd Street, walked one block, and entered a five-story building on 23rd Street between Seventh and Eighth avenues.

I waited several minutes, then inspected the cramped lobby. Yes, Suite E read DAN WU ENTERPRISES. What an uninspiring building for the office for a celebrity chef! One would think he'd have a glass palace in Chinatown—something beautiful and exotic.

But when I went back onto the street and looked up, I realized the building wasn't really all that shabby—clearly, the inside had recently been renovated into what appeared to be gallery spaces with massive high windows.

It was a little past nine-thirty. I crossed 23rd Street in the middle of the block and sat down at the counter of a small coffee shop, from which I could see the entrance of the building that Pallister had entered. I ordered a cup of coffee and a small orange juice.

How long would he be in there? What if he stayed all day? The thought sobered me greatly. I had begun the surveillance on a "high"—not really having thought it out carefully. It was a way to help Sonny surreptitiously, and a way to show him he couldn't order me around. And of course it was for poor disappeared Millie, wherever she might be in all her tabby splendor.

When I started out that morning, it had never even occurred to me that Jack Pallister might simply put in a full day's work. If that did happen, it would mean seven hours in a coffee shop for me, drinking cup after cup so as not to be asked to leave. That would be intolerable.

But has there ever been an ex-actor who could work a full day? They simply can't. They're too unstable.

I ordered a toasted corn muffin to supplement my rather desperate speculations. Fifteen minutes later, those speculations had become irrelevant.

Jack Pallister emerged from the building, looking at his watch. He started to walk west, very fast, on 23rd Street.

I flew out of the coffee shop and followed on the opposite side of the street, holding on to my straw hat so it wouldn't fly off. I almost had to run to keep sight of him.

He went down into the Eighth Avenue subway station on the north side of 23rd Street. I descended on the south side. He boarded the second car of an E train. I boarded the third car, keeping him in view through the window between cars.

My heart was pounding. I had gotten onto the subway train so fast that I didn't even know which way it was heading. Then I saw the local stops moving by. We were definitely going uptown. The train pulled into 34th Street. He didn't get off. And he didn't get off at any of the subsequent Manhattan stops, so I knew we were going to Queens.

Twenty minutes later he exited the train at Continental Avenue in Forest Hills. He was almost running. He turned onto Austin Street, then onto a second side street. He leaped up the three stone steps of a small brick house, rang the bell, and vanished inside.

I moved closer to the house to read the small sign on the door. It read:

DR. M. L. MEI
ACUPUNCTURIST
HONG KONG TRAINED
HOURS: 9:45 A.M.—3:45 P.M.
MON–FRI

I felt like an utter fool. The high adventure of the chase had come crashing down. Pallister had gone out to Queens like a man possessed, only to get a few tiny needles stuck in him.

I walked away from the house and stared at a small, unhealthy-looking ginkgo tree. As I was trying to figure out where on the block I should continue with my now deflated surveillance scheme, I noticed another individual walk up to the house and ring the bell. He was wearing very strange clothes: a three-quarter-length black tunic, over tan pants. And on his head was perched one of those little four-cornered pillbox hats.

I couldn't place the mode of dress.

Fifteen minutes later, a different man emerged. He, too, was wearing that exotic dress.

Indian? Pakistani? No.

Then I remembered where I had seen it: in a movie about Sukarno, the one-time President of Indonesia, a brutal dictator.

Then I remembered the cartons of dried mushrooms and ginger root Sonny had shown me in the storeroom of Dan Wu's restaurant.

I couldn't recall the name of the port city stenciled on the cartons, but Sonny had said the city was in Sumatra, and I knew that Sumatra was part of the Indonesian archipelago.

Suddenly I was wide-awake, and very much interested in that little brick house. It was too strong and too strange a coincidence to let it pass by. It had to be explored.

Forty-five minutes after he had entered, Jack Pallister walked out. He seemed calm and content. The acupuncture treatment had obviously done wonders. He could now remember his lines. He headed toward the subway.

I let him travel alone. The moment he vanished from sight I climbed the steps and rang the bell. A buzzer buzzed, and I stepped inside.

I was standing in a small vestibule. Beyond the vestibule was a waiting room filled with red-lacquered Chinese-style furniture and four patients—three male and one female. Two of the males wore the distinctive Indonesian garb.

A door on the far side of the waiting room opened slowly, and a gnomish Chinese man with tufts of white hair stared out at me. Then he slipped through the door, closed it softly behind him, and approached me.

"I am Dr. Mei," he announced, executing a somewhat deferential half-bow, as if I were of the greatest importance and was honoring his humble establishment with my presence. "How may I be of service?"

His manner brought back to me a conversation I'd had with Sonny, in which I had asked what secret the Chinese possess that enables them to exist together so amicably in incredibly crowded areas. In New York's Chinatown, for example, the most densely populated area of the city, one is never jostled on the street. Sonny replied that the secret is simple: Chinese people are taught from infancy to act as if everyone they come into contact with is a social superior—whether or not that is the case. This applies to everyone, from the dregs of society to the exalted ones. What a wondrous method for reducing rudeness and jostling on crowded city streets!

Dentist-like, Dr. Mei was wearing a starched white coat. It was buttoned from top to bottom. He was also wearing bedroom slippers.

"I'm sorry to barge in like this, Dr. Mei," I apologized. "I just wanted an appointment, and couldn't find your number in the phone book."

"But I am in the phone book," he affirmed, and then smiled as if it really were of no significance either way. "I have a patient now, and there are others waiting. Can you tell me briefly why you wish my help?"

I thought quickly. "Leg cramps, Dr. Mei. They come suddenly and disable me. I've been to a dozen doctors, and none of them has helped me."

He smiled and patted me on the arm. "To whom am I speaking?"

"Hayley Mills," I lied.

"Come in two days' time, Miss Mills. At ten o'clock in the morning."

"Thank you, Dr. Mei," I said, and walked out.

I hurried to the subway, then decided against that mode of transportation. I contemplated a cab, but that was simply too extravagant. Instead I crossed the wide avenue called Queens Boulevard and boarded a very slow bus headed into Manhattan.

I had no idea where all this would lead, but I knew I had done the right thing. If Dr. Mei turned out to be a dead end, then I would go back to Jack Pallister. Besides, it was time I finally found out just what acupuncture was all about.

The bus dropped me off on 60th Street and Second Avenue in Manhattan. I took the downtown bus to 28th Street and picked up some fruit and paper towels.

When I reached my house I put the package down to rest outside before beginning the long climb to my apartment.

A strong, cool breeze was beginning to blow. I closed my eyes and let it caress my face. I wanted to be with Sonny very much.

Finally, I picked up the package and opened the lobby door.

Suddenly, a terrible pain went up and down my lower leg.

A second later I heard a loud noise. And then another noise. And another.

I fell to one knee. My straw hat fell off.

I reached down to retrieve it, and my fingers felt something warm and sticky.

I knew then I had been shot. People started to scream, but I couldn't see them. I felt giddy, almost happy. Then the world began to spin very fast.

14

Millie was lovely in a white wedding dress, her red tail held high, a black garter around it.

Bushy was resplendent in tux and top hat.

The best man was Pancho, shoeless but otherwise impeccably attired, his dull gray coat brushed to a shine and his half-tail combed out.

The minister was Dan Wu. And his assistant, holding the wedding ring on an acupuncture needle, was Dr. Mei.

I was watching the ceremony from outside the church, through a stained-glass window. My grandmother was in a pew, holding the hand of a little Eurasian boy.

A naked piano player began to play and sing, "Now we gather in the chapel. . . ."

Then I woke up.

I was lying on a hospital table that had been pushed against one long wall in the New York Hospital emergency room. At my toes was another table, occupied by a large comatose woman, lying on her side. On the table at my head there lay a thin Hispanic man, with tubes sticking in him. And Sonny Hoving was holding my hand tightly. He looked very agitated.

"What happened, Sonny?"

He tried to be amusing. "I just can't leave you

alone for a minute, can I, Alice? Well, the precinct cops think you stepped into the middle of a dispute among geeks from that methadone clinic near Bellevue."

Then I remembered the blood. And my straw hat. I sat up quickly and stared at my left leg.

"You're okay, Alice. You're fine! The bullets just grazed your heel, just enough to break the skin through the shoe. They slid along . . . like bowling balls, but they really didn't enter. A lot of blood, little damage."

I wiggled my toes. Everything was numb. I could see a piece of white gauze taped to the base of the heel.

"Why did I lose consciousness?"

"Shock, I suppose. It happens, Alice. Nothing to be ashamed of. Sometimes the sight of one's own blood is overpowering."

I hadn't seen the blood, but I remembered touching it. I remembered the stickiness.

Sonny started to kiss the inside of my hand. "When I heard what happened I almost went crazy," he said. "I can't afford to have anything happen to you now, Alice. I really don't know what I would do if you vanished."

"Mourn, like everyone else," I noted.

"Maybe you better move off your block, Alice."

"My block is fine . . . and safe."

"Right!" Sonny said sarcastically.

"I wasn't shot by drug dealers," I said matter-of-factly, but with authority.

"You saw the shooter?" he asked, incredulous.

"No."

"What, then? You're not making sense, Alice."

"It was a warning."

He threw up his hands in a childish gesture of impatience.

I continued: "I had been following Jack Pallister."

"You *what*!" he barked angrily, then turned and walked away from me to contain his anger . . . and walked back.

"I *asked* you not to do that," he said menacingly.

"Well, I did."

He took my hand again, this time pressing it against his face. His look was imploring, gentle, pleading. At that moment, and for the first time, I realized that Sonny Hoving loved me. It made me happy yet also strangely uncomfortable, as if I were playing a part not right for me. My leading man was too young . . . too provincial . . . too NYPD, in spite of himself.

"You have to listen to me, Alice. Dan Wu is a very dangerous man. And if you rile his worker bees, you are going to get stung bad."

"He may be a dangerous man, this Dan Wu, or he may just be a very good cook."

"I warn you: Don't be a fool, Alice."

I closed my eyes and pretended to sleep.

A few hours later he took me home, and then he left. I tested my heel gingerly, walking from one end of the living room to the other, from the window to the door, very slowly, watched by a very confused Maine coon cat.

The heel hurt only when I put the full weight of my body on it. Quickly I found an alternate mode of ambulation, one that no doubt appeared to the onlooker as if I had survived some childhood ordeal that left me with one shortened leg.

The next morning I evaluated my options.

Option number one: Forget the whole matter, and cancel my appointment with Dr. Mei.

Option number two: Cancel the appointment with Dr. Mei, but put surveillance on him, by me.

Why surveillance on Mei? Because the thread progressed from Wu to Pallister to Mei. And coloring that thread was the Indonesian connection: cartons of dried food from Sumatra in Dan Wu's restaurant, and Indonesians waiting for acupuncture treatment from a doctor whom Pallister used, or at least visited.

The available options were clear. Other things were not so clear. My motives, for example. Why, if I was still entranced by my young man, did I continue to go against his wish that I should butt out? Was it really to help him? Was it for Millie?

And equally unclear was the reason I was not frightened. After all, someone had shot real live bullets at me—and there was no doubt in my mind that it was a warning. Just like Sonny had warned me to stay out of the case . . . only a little more malevolent.

Why hadn't the shooting frightened me? Oh, it must have frightened me at the time, when I'd felt my own blood and fainted. But afterward, it was an abstraction; I simply had no fear of the person or persons who had orchestrated it.

Truth be told, I am a physical coward. Going to the dentist, for example, usually requires six weeks of meditation on my part on the unseemliness of tooth loss for an actress, before I'm able to get up and go.

And even my grandmother, who raised me, used to crow about how I'd been an absolute joy as a child because, unlike many children, I didn't court danger; didn't spend my time looking for swinging doors and gates and deep ponds and irate beasts.

It was a mystery.

Anyway, I chose option two. I was enmeshed. I could not retreat. I had to get far enough to at least see the light at the other end, and a red tabby kitchen cat basking in that light, her long tail swinging.

It was a hard-bitten decision for a wimp like me to come to, and for several moments, as I perfected my bruised-heel gait in my apartment, it brought me a good bit of amusement.

Was I becoming yet another exemplar of that new breed of devil-may-care women who light up the current cinema—tough-talking, fearless, aggressive, able to talk sports and booze and sex and death as well as any male rogue?

God, I hoped not! Those women appall me.

Like any other actress, I could have gone on and on with explorations of motive. All I really knew was that I was determined to follow Dr. Mei.

It was easier to follow Mei than Pallister. Dr. Mei's office hours lasted until three forty-five. That was when the surveillance started. It was cut-and-dried.

I showed up not merely with a rented car, but a rented car and *driver*. The charge was seventeen dollars per hour for both man and machine. The machine was an enormous Chrysler. The man was an Egyptian named, exotically, Omar Mekheil.

It was an extravagant move, a move that emptied one-quarter of my fragile checking account—but forty-one-year-old women in befuddled love with younger men do not act rationally.

Particularly if said forty-one-year-old woman considers herself a criminal investigator of great gifts.

And if she can't get the memory of a darling tabby kitchen cat out of her mind.

And if she has a bruised heel.

And if her usual rent-a-car companion, one Tony Basillio, is no longer in communication with her because her heart has been driven away, a new man behind the wheel.

Omar and I sat in the surveillance car, silently, across from Dr. Mei's house. Omar was snoozing. When I had told him that we would be following one individual wherever he went, he appeared neither surprised nor interested.

The last patient left at four-fifteen.

Dr. Mei himself emerged at four forty-one.

He was wearing a business suit and carrying a large, old-fashioned leather briefcase with elaborate straps—the kind crazed music teachers used to carry.

I tapped Omar on the shoulder. He woke and started the engine. Dr. Mei walked toward the corner and unlocked and entered a new, blue Ford Escort. He started the engine and pulled out. We followed in our huge black Chrysler.

Dr. Mei drove steadily through the streets of Queens. He never exceeded twenty-five miles per hour. When he turned into a wide thoroughfare with Asian-owned stores on both sides, he slowed to about ten miles per hour.

"What neighborhood is this?" I asked Omar.

"Flushing," Omar replied.

Dr. Mei, who seemed like such a gentle, law-abiding man, astonished me then by brazenly double-parking his car and walking into an Asian pharmacy with his briefcase.

Through my backseat window, I could see clearly what was transpiring in the store.

Dr. Mei waited patiently for the counter man, who was obviously busy filling a prescription. Then he came out from behind the counter and bowed ceremoniously, Dr. Mei likewise. Then they shook hands. After a few moments of what seemed to be animated conversation, Dr. Mei opened his briefcase, removed a small brown paper bag, and handed it to the pharmacist . . . who, in turn, half bowed again, and vanished with the bag into the rear of the store.

A few minutes later the pharmacist returned with a small white envelope, which he handed to Dr. Mei, who placed it in his briefcase and did up all the straps.

End of drama. Dr. Mei returned to his car.

He made two other stops in Flushing. Then two in Jackson Heights. Then two in Astoria. The scenario was always the same: an Asian-owned pharmacy; a brown paper bag; a white envelope.

Then Dr. Mei drove back to Forest Hills, parked his car, and vanished into his house.

"Well, miss?" My Egyptian-American cab driver queried, obviously hoping the expedition was over—regardless of the seventeen an hour. Traffic in Queens was even more nerve-racking than in Manhattan.

I held up my hand, signifying that I was thinking. What had happened was so simple I just couldn't believe it. I couldn't believe how uncomplicated it had turned out to be. It was right out in the open. Whatever was in those brown paper bags was some kind of contraband.

I felt no triumph, no exultation, no sense of accomplishment at all.

I had merely witnessed a series of murky—and probably criminal—transactions.

It was like the feeling an actress gets when she confronts a famous director for the first time and that director, instead of uttering the expected profundity, the theatrical gem, merely says, "I like your shoes."

Yes, It was like that.

"Take me to 12th and University, in Manhattan," I ordered. Omar the Obedient drove on.

15

"You can't keep showing up at my apartment without an appointment," Sonny quipped. "It looks bad to my other women."

I smiled at him as he stood, nonchalantly naked, in his doorway.

"What's so funny?"

He had just emerged from the shower, and was chewing a sliver of honeydew melon.

"I'm smiling because you're what every woman should have."

"Truer words never spoken," he agreed gallantly, and ushered me in.

I kissed him on the mouth and eyes. He was beautiful to look at, and beautiful to touch. He dropped the honeydew rind on the floor.

"What's all *this* about?" he asked, startled.

For a moment, a brief but very intense moment, I thought of rescinding my temporary ban on eros. But the moment passed.

We walked arm in arm to the bed. The small apartment had a soft glow. We sat down. He put his hand in mine, and I put both our hands chastely in my lap.

"How is your heel?" he asked.

"A bit stiff."

"Any pain?"

"No. No pain. But I did spend the day riding instead of walking."

He looked pensive.

"I took a car ride to Queens," I said.

"People do all kinds of strange things after they've been shot."

"And when I was out there . . . wouldn't you know that I found myself in front of an acupuncturist's office that Jack Pallister often visited? A man, coincidently, with a lot of Indonesian patients."

Sonny started to shake his head, ruefully. He took his hand away.

"An lo and behold," I continued in my storyteller's mode, "this acupuncturist, Dr. Mei, walks out and gets into his car. And just out of curiosity I start to follow him."

"Damn!" Sonny exclaimed, leaving the bed and walking to the window. "What's the matter with you, Alice? I keep asking that question. Are you crazy? We both agreed that you wouldn't do this anymore!"

For the first time since I had met him I felt a flash of enmity toward him. He was so handsome—and so screwed-up. It was strange how this affair had progressed: from a moment of loneliness to a moment of recognition to a moment of fascination to a moment of passion to a moment of intimacy. But they had always been mere moments, always precarious.

"I thought, Sonny," I said archly, "that I was the great love of your life."

"You are."

"Then try and act like it," I replied, realizing that I was starting to sound like his maiden aunt.

"Come here, Sonny, and sit down. I want to show you something."

He sat down, leery. I handed him a piece of paper.

"What is this?"

"The names and addresses of seven pharmacies in Queens. Each one Asian-owned. And in each one, Jack Pallister's acupuncturist made a trade. A brown paper bag for a white envelope."

"Do you know what was in the brown paper bag?" Sonny was beginning to pay attention.

"No. But I can guess what was in the white envelope."

"Money?"

"Money."

Sonny stared at the paper, exhaling deeply. "I find it hard to believe," he said in a quiet, reflective tone, "that after all this time banging my head against a stone wall trying to nail Dan Wu . . . you come blithely along, sashaying through a field of wildflowers, and start to follow one of his flunkies, who leads you to a needle doctor, and—*poof!*—you witness seven bald-faced transactions involving something dirty."

"I'm afraid you are going to have to believe it, Sonny. It happened."

Sonny sprang off the bed. "Damn it, Alice, you did it! Good work! There's only one problem. We're ten cents short, if you know what I mean. I mean, if they're dealing in something heavy, those pharmacists are going to keep their mouths shut. If they don't roll over on Mei, he won't roll over on Pallister. And Pallister won't implicate Wu."

"And Rothwax is a rough man to work for," I added.

"Exactly. There's just not enough for me to move on."

"I think I have a solution."

His eyes widened. He seemed to have become very thankful for my help, but more then a bit skeptical about accepting any more Nestleton first aid. I had to be gentle and self-effacing.

"I thought maybe we could trick Jack Pallister and Dr. Mei into making some statements."

"How are we going to do that?"

"Did you ever hear of The Bushy and Pancho Freight Forwarding Company—truckers extraordinaire?"

"No," he said with a laugh, "but I assume that since your cats are the sole owners, it operates out of your apartment."

"It does, Sonny. Now, assume that a bill of lading on Bushy and Pancho's letterhead is sent to Jack Pallister. It informs him that an effort was made to deliver to Dan Wu's restaurant some crates of dried foodstuffs from Sumatra."

"But the restaurant is closed," Sonny interjected.

"Exactly. Where should the crates be delivered? My guess is that Pallister will have them delivered to Mei."

"Yes. If the crates contain the contraband . . . if that's the way they're bringing it in—whatever 'it' is. But then what?"

"Then you enhance the trick with one of the NYPD's technological marvels."

"You mean a bug?"

"Yes. A listening device right in the dried mushrooms."

Sonny slapped his hands together with glee, like a child. "Beautiful, Alice! Beautiful!"

"And you don't have to go through RETRO at all. You don't have to tell Rothwax a thing. You can use some of the crates still in the restaurant. And the phony bill of lading you can print up for twenty-five bucks. Only the bug may be a problem."

"That's no problem at all," he said sharply. "If I followed department procedure on all cases, I wouldn't clear a single one of them."

He stared at me for a long time, admiringly. Of course, what I didn't tell him was that we each had a different agenda. He wanted smuggled contraband tied to Dan Wu and the restaurant killing. I wanted Millie, first and foremost. What he didn't know wouldn't hurt him.

Sonny rejoined me on the bed. His eyes were alive. "You are one impressive woman, Alice Nestleton."

"Well, Sonny," I said softly, stroking his black hair, "we older woman are sometimes even wiser out of bed than we are in."

We both began to laugh.

16

How many times did we argue bitterly in the next seventy-two hours as we closed the trap on them? Oh, many times.

After Sonny took two of the crates of dried food from the shut-down restaurant and stacked them against one wall of his apartment, we argued about whether two crates were really enough to bait the trap.

After Sonny had the phony bill of lading printed up and sent to Pallister, we argued about the quality of the printing.

After Pallister called my number and, not recognizing my disguised voice, instructed that the crates be delivered to Dr. Mei, we argued about the accent I had used.

After Sonny had wired the crates for sound, we argued about whether he had put the bugs in the right place.

The fact is, we were as wired as the crates.

It was as if Sonny and I were part of a performance group, ready to foist on an audience a dramatic production of great power and beauty, and the only way to ensure the quality of that performance was to fight like cats and dogs before the curtain went up. Yes, things surely do get out of proportion.

Anyway, Sonny delivered the cartons on a Tuesday afternoon, dressed in his conception of a trucker's getup; then he sat in his unmarked car across the street from Dr. Mei, waiting to record.

I waited in his apartment.

Hours passed. I listened to some of Sonny's Muddy Waters records, then looked for some Eastern music that would better reflect his Eurasian background. I couldn't find any, so I opted for some Richard Pryor comedy. Pryor is a very funny man, but I didn't laugh. For some reason, comedy routines rarely make me laugh.

Besides, I was nervous. A thousand things could go wrong. Pallister could simply not show up at Dr. Mei's for some reason. The "bug" might be defective. And worst of all, the whole enterprise might be based on a chimera—the transactions I had witnessed in the Asian pharmacies might simply have been exotic, not criminal.

I turned the record off and waited in silence.

Then I had a sudden yearning to cook for Sonny, so that when he came home I could feed him. Ah, the pull of domesticity. I rushed to his refrigerator and opened it. Inside was a large can of pineapple juice, one exhausted tomato, and three chocolate bars. The line "Come live with me and be my love" popped into my head and I went back to the bed and lay down.

He arrived at twenty past nine. Home was the hunter, home from the hill. He looked loose and easy in his trucker's outfit.

The smile was from ear to ear. He held up a tiny cassette with a triumphant flourish, then took my hand and led me in some obscure victory dance—a kind of stomp, actually.

Was it really possible that this crazed hoofer

was a hardened NYPD detective, and I a cynical actress turned cat-sitter?

Then, happily, he ended the dance abruptly, and placed a finger to his lips for silence.

I wouldn't have dreamed of speaking.

He put the tiny tape into the cassette player on the floor, snapping it into place with precision, then motioned for me to lie on the floor with my ear next to the speaker. We both did.

It was scratchy and bumpy and low. But it was audible. I could hear them talking. After three listens we knew what they had said.

MEI: This was most unwise . . . sending them here.

PALLISTER: Easy for you to say. I didn't have a choice. I couldn't take the chance of them floating around.

MEI: What was the rush? We weren't expecting any more.

PALLISTER: You're getting senile, old friend. Don't you remember that the last shipment was a few crates short?

MEI: And these are the crates?

PALLISTER: How the hell should I know? Maybe. Maybe not. Things get lost. Things get found. What did we have to lose? I covered our tracks.

The moment he uttered those words I squeezed Sonny's arm—the bit about covering tracks could only refer to Pallister shooting me in the heel. What else could he be talking about?

Next there came the sound of crates being opened, followed by inchoate curses. Then:

PALLISTER: Not a damn thing!

MEI: Your greed has turned you into a pack rat.

PALLISTER: Who are you calling names, you goddamn hypocrite? If these had been those lost crates, you would have been dancing on your acupuncture table. We're talking a lot of money.

MEI: There will be more.

PALLISTER: You know, I'm developing a very strong dislike for you.

MEI: Good. Now maybe you will never again reroute one of these crates to my house.

The sound died. I sat up. How often does one hear such a brilliantly resolved one-act play? Sonny was grinning like the proverbial Cheshire.

"It's enough to get a search warrant! Oh, yes! It's enough to see what the slick Dr. Mei is hiding in his pantry!"

I felt happy because Sonny was happy. But where was Millie? Where was any mention of poor vanished Millie? Where was any mention of the restaurant shooting?

Sonny was now close to me on the floor, nuzzling his face into my neck. He whispered, "And I formally invite you, against all existing departmental regulations, to witness the execution of a search warrant on the premises of Dr. Mei." He kissed me. Then he added: "Dress is optional."

17

At seven-twenty in the misty morning, Sonny Hoving, three other NYPD detectives assigned to RETRO, and I walked up to Dr. Mei's front door.

I had been introduced to them as someone vaguely attached to the DA's office to monitor procedures in warrant searches. They greeted me and then ignored me.

Sonny was elaborately officious, holding his badge high before the sleepy, berobed Dr. Mei, who had opened the door after a full two minutes of buzzer ringing. Sonny then thrust the warrant paper at him as if it were a long-awaited gift.

When Dr. Mei saw me, he seemed to awaken, groggily. Clearly he remembered me from somewhere, but couldn't place me. He kept staring at me as we all politely pushed our way inside.

Then I saw a flicker of what could only be fear on the good doctor's face. As if he had somehow, suddenly, tied in the strange tall lady with Pallister and the crates—and an acupuncture appointment that was never kept.

Once inside, no words were spoken by the detectives. It was a small two-family house, and they seemed to know exactly what to do and where to go. I wondered if there exists somewhere a school that teaches police officers how to search thoroughly and quickly. If so, these cops surely graduated magna cum laude. They looked over, under, and in everything. They ran their hands over walls, ledges, and carpets. All done with a minimum of noise and dislocation.

They tapped every piece of exposed plumbing and pipe with ballpoint pens.

Yet even though they seemed to be searching with a manic energy, they were quite gentle with objects that could have been of sentimental or financial value to Dr. Mei. It was a most impressive performance, and I was truly mesmerized by it.

Sonny stayed with Dr. Mei in the waiting room. I flitted about, always returning to keep Sonny company. From time to time Sonny said something to Dr. Mei in Chinese, but he was never answered.

One of the detectives stuck his head in and signaled that he had found nothing so far. Sonny gestured to him to stay with Mei, and gestured to me that I should accompany him.

We walked downstairs into the basement. It was one of those semi-finished basements, absolutely bare of furniture and objects except for the spic-and-span oil heater.

"It looks like a small ballroom dancing studio," I said, looking at the highly waxed linoleum floor.

"Or Tai-Chi," Sonny commented.

He circled the basement carefully. The only spots that could have hidden something were the exposed ceiling beams. He ran his hands along all of them—nothing.

"It smells clean down here, doesn't it?" he noted.

I agreed. Very clean. But Dr. Mei was a physician of sorts—cleanliness was to be expected.

Then I said, "It's really too bad we don't know what we're looking for."

"We know what we're looking for, Alice."

"Which is?"

"Something that's illegal, easy to carry, and readily convertible to cash."

I must have been very much in love with Sonny, because after he made that rather pedestrian remark, I felt a surge of pride in him. I wanted to show the whole world how smart my platonic lover was.

"Let's try the garage," Sonny suggested.

A door connected the basement and the garage, the latter being little more than a cement square with a tin door opening onto the street.

Along the walls were three large workbenches with aluminum folding legs, various implements, tools, and hoses piled haphazardly atop them.

In one corner of the garage were two bicycles.

That was all.

"I wonder why Dr. Mei parks his car on the street instead of in here," Sonny mused.

"Maybe he doesn't like opening and closing that ugly door."

Sonny nodded, and began to go carefully through the objects on the workbenches. Then he checked the legs and underpinnings.

"Nothing," he said to me, standing up and stepping back. He had a grim smile on his face.

Then his eyes fell on the bikes.

"Pretty bikes," he said admiringly but grudgingly, as if those associated with Dan Wu couldn't possibly make beautiful and functional selections in their lives.

After a moment's study, I decided that the bikes really were rather pretty. They were the new breed called "mountain bikes" and at first glance they appeared brutish, with their thick wheels and squat profiles. But upon second glance they were oddly satisfying to the eye. They must have been frightfully expensive. The word FUJI stood out on the frame, and I'd heard somewhere that Fuji bikes are always pricey.

Sonny circled the standing bikes.

"We Asians dearly love our bicycles," he said, and I couldn't tell whether he was serious or joking.

Then he squatted down on his heels until he was easily, perfectly balanced with no visible means of support.

As he stared at the bikes he simply sat there, just as Chinese kitchen workers relaxing outside their restaurant do, talking or eating. It was one of those revealing moments. For the first time I realized that in some part of his being Sonny was, indeed, truly Chinese. And I loved him all the more for it.

"Did you know, Alice, that if it hadn't been for the bicycle, the Vietnamese never would have destroyed the French army at Dienbienphu?"

"No, I didn't know that, Sonny."

"The French thought the Vietnamese couldn't transport artillery pieces and ammunition through the mountains and threaten their base. But they could, and did. On bicycles. Amazing, isn't it? They reinforced the bike frames, and each rider carried some four hundred pounds strapped to his bike over the steep mountain trails. He stood up. "Amazing," he repeated. Then he changed the subject abruptly.

"How old do you think Dr. Mei is?"

"To me he looks at least seventy."

"I agree. At least seventy, maybe seventy-five. Now that's strange, isn't it?"

"You mean it's strange for a man that age to ride a bike? No, I don't think so. A lot of senior citizens ride bikes now."

"Not that. I mean strange that he would buy *Fuji* bikes."

"What's strange about that? I thought they were top-rated."

"They are. But most Chinese people over a certain age have a deep and abiding resentment against the Japanese for the atrocities they committed when they occupied China before and during World War Two. They tend not to buy Japanese goods. Just like many older Jewish people won't purchase German-made products."

He kept looking at the bikes. I didn't know how to respond to what he was saying, so I kept silent.

Then he moved quickly, violently. I flinched involuntarily. He pulled a small saw from the workbench, strode to one of the bikes, and cut clean through one of the beautiful Fuji bicycle tires—the front one.

Out fell a small paper bag.

"That's it!" I shouted. "That's the same kind of bag Dr. Mei gave to the pharmacists!"

Sonny squeezed the tire. More small brown paper bags fastened with rubber bands dropped out.

Sonny picked up a bag and feverishly tried to remove the tightly wound rubber band, then just violently ripped the top of the bag off.

An ugly gray powder poured out of the ripped bag onto the garage floor.

We both stared down at it. A funny, almost musty odor enveloped us.

Sonny reached down and brought some of the powder up, rubbing it between his fingers as a look of astonishment began to spread across his face.

"You are looking at five hundred dollars an ounce," he said softly, almost reverently.

I stared incredulously at the evil-smelling powder. How could something like that be worth five hundred an ounce? It wasn't gold. It wasn't cocaine. It wasn't heroin.

"What is it, Sonny?"

"Powdered rhino horn. Old Asian men will kill for it. They think it cures impotence. They think it gives them their sexual youth back—erections unlimited. But it really doesn't do a damn thing except take all their money."

He dusted the all-but-priceless powder off his fingers.

"And it's illegal. It's against the law to ship or export or sell or even possess, because it can only be obtained by poaching protected rhinos."

He began to pace, talking excitedly as he moved. "It all makes sense now! That Lapidus, the bad guy in the photo with Wu, put Wu and his people in touch with Sumatran rhino poachers. The horn was ground down in Sumatra and shipped to Dan Wu's restaurant in New York in crates of dried mushrooms and ginger root. Then it was packaged and retailed in New York and probably elsewhere by Mei and Pallister. And the shooting in the restaurant was obviously a warning to Wu from the established Hong Kong families to get out of this lucrative scam—which has been theirs, traditionally."

Sonny returned to the little pile of powder and spat bitterly into it, his contempt and hatred almost frightening me. "I'm finally going to get that bastard. Aren't I?"

He was talking about Dan Wu. But I was thinking about Millie. Who was going to get *her*?

18

Dan Wu seemed to be much younger, this time, than when I had seen him briefly at the Waldorf. He was still white-haired and elegant, of course, but the moment one studied him up close one realized that he had to be twenty years younger than he looked at first. It made him all the more impressive.

He sat behind an enormous, mushroom-shaped wood desk. The desk top was so thin that it seemed one could peel an orange against it. On top of the desk were only two objects: a snow-white legal pad, and a single pencil, perfectly sharpened. I felt very much that I was in the court of a great gourmet chef.

On the wall behind Dan Wu was a humorous blown-up photo of him, showing him dropping a wok during one of his television shows. The wok has slipped from his grasp and spiraled upward, the ingredients tumbling every which way. Dan Wu is staring at the fleeing wok with a look of total perplexity. It is a wonderful photo.

The room itself was very large, and just one of the many recently renovated, whitewashed spaces that belied the shabby exterior of the West 23rd Street building that housed Dan Wu Enterprises.

Dan Wu had greeted Sonny and me warmly, as

if we were old friends. An underling had served us pear juice in tiny enamel mugs.

He kept smiling at us tenderly, in his beautiful dark green polo shirt and lighter green blazer, with dull silver buttons and the hint of an even lighter green handkerchief peeking out from the blazer pocket. Everything about the man was impeccable.

As for Sonny, the mere presence of Dan Wu enraged him. His body seemed to be coiled like a spring. I was afraid that, as he sipped the pear juice, he would bite through the enamel.

Wu beamed at me. "My associate, Jack Pallister, has been talking about you constantly since he met you at the Waldorf."

I was about to reply, "You mean he told you how he likes to shoot actresses in the heel?" But I said nothing.

Wu continued: "What was the word he kept using? Ah, yes—'cognoscenti.' He kept saying that the real cognoscenti know just how talented you are."

"As a cat-sitter?" I asked coyly.

He laughed. "I'm sure you have many outstanding talents, Miss Nestleton. But I believe Jack was referring to the theater."

His voice was modulated and mellow. I would happily pay to hear such a voice reading even a parking ticket.

Then the world-famous chef turned to Sonny: "Tell me," he said, "did you enjoy this year's Jade Society dinner?"

"Why don't we cut out all this garbage!" Sonny barked savagely, hunching over in his chair. "You know why we're here. Because your two associates—Pallister and Mei—are in custody.

They were dealing in contraband—rhino horn. Smuggling it in and distributing it. And the whole damn ugly mess leads right back to you and your restaurant."

Dan Wu smiled at Sonny as if Sonny were a child. "I know no one by the name of Mei," he said.

Sonny grinned wickedly. He waited, his eyes boring into Wu. Wu returned the stare for what seemed the longest time, then sighed and leaned back in his chair. He sighed again, this time enormously.

"Very well," he said, "I shall tell you what I know."

He paused, playing with the pencil, tapping the end of it on the legal pad. Then he continued.

"About a year ago I discovered what Jack was doing. I was shocked and appalled. I tried to dissuade him, but he is a very stubborn man. Finally, I met in secret with that man Lapidus and, quite frankly, offered him money if he would end his smuggling relationship with Jack. Lapidus refused. He was murdered before I could speak to him again. Jack swore to me, after I kept on nagging him, that he had stopped. But I really didn't believe him. It didn't matter. There was nothing I could do. So I did nothing."

Sonny shook his head disgustedly. "You don't really expect me to believe that fairy tale."

Dan Wu replied, "I am telling you the truth."

Sonny snapped back, "You're a liar! You ran the stuff in! You sold it! You profited from it!"

"I have told you the truth."

Sonny stood up, grabbed my hand, and pulled me up also.

"Hear me good, Mr. Wu. One of your associates

is going to roll over. Sooner or later. And you're going to be cooking in Atlanta, or whatever federal country club they send you to. And a lot of people are going to be very happy."

Sonny kept hold of my hand as we walked through the hallway to the elevator. "Does he think I'm an idiot? Did he really think I would believe that story?"

At the elevator I panicked. I realized that if I didn't speak to Dan Wu now about Millie, I might never get the chance. It wasn't something I could tell Sonny, so I lied to him.

"My purse, Sonny! I left my purse in Dan Wu's office." I shook my hand loose from his grasp and headed back down the hallway. "Hold the elevator for me. I'll be back in a sec."

Dan Wu looked up casually as I entered his office again.

"I have to ask you about Millie. I want to know what happened to her," I blurted out.

"Who is Millie?" he asked quietly.

"A cat. Your kitchen cat. The cat in your Tribeca restaurant."

He stared at me for a full thirty seconds without answering. It was a most peculiar look. I simply couldn't fathom it, but it made me uncomfortable.

Then he asked, "You saw a cat in my restaurant?"

Was he pulling my leg? What was going on?

"Of course I saw a cat. A big red tabby. She was lying on one of the high shelves in the kitchen."

"Was the cat looking at the moon?" he asked.

"No. The cat was looking down at the customers."

Again there was a long silence. The conversation was unreal. Was he serious about a cat looking at the moon?

Then he said, "What you saw, perhaps, was a dragon."

"A what?"

"A dragon. Perhaps you saw a dragon."

"Please, I don't have time to play with you. The cat . . . your kitchen cat . . . vanished the night of the shooting. What happened to her? Is she okay?"

"I know of no cat," he said calmly.

"Are you telling me there was no cat in that restaurant the night of the shooting? Are you telling me I didn't see a red cat?"

"I know of no cat."

For the first time I got some sense of why Sonny hated this man. He was either a criminal or a pathological liar, or just too elliptical to be believed about anything.

Furious, I turned on my heel and started back toward the elevator.

"Miss Nestleton!" he called out.

I stopped walking but didn't turn around to face him.

"You seem to be rushing from place to place, Miss Nestleton. You seem to be chasing cats and people. Why don't you slow down?"

There was genuine concern in his voice. For me. I turned and stared at him. What a strange man!

"Don't you know, Miss Nestleton, that without going outside your door, you can understand everything on earth and in heaven?"

"Right now, Mr. Wu, all I'm interested in is your kitchen cat, Millie."

"Yes, that's what you say," he replied. He stared

hard at me. For a moment I saw something trapped in his eyes, an impulse of contrition or shame that he was trying to communicate to me silently.

"Good-bye, Mr. Wu," I said formally.

"Good-bye, Miss Nestleton. You are always welcome here."

I walked quickly back to the elevator where Sonny waited, impatiently, his foot jammed against the bottom of the elevator door to keep it open.

"Well, did you find it?"

"Find what?"

"Your purse."

"Oh. . . . No. No. It turns out I didn't bring one with me after all."

19

The buzzer was ringing. Incessantly. Wildly. Beats and bleats and rolls. Songs. Snatches of songs. A full orchestra.

Was a crazy person downstairs this time?

Even Bushy, who was usually oblivious to that buzzer, seemed to take notice. He sat up and gave a few of those darting, intelligent glances that seem to say "Take heed!"

It was only eight-twenty in the morning. I was expecting no deliveries so I reasoned it out feebly, still in the grip of my traditional morning stupor. It was either a psychotic from some local halfway house . . . or, heaven help me, Tony Basillio making a surprise appearance to deal with my infidelity . . . or Sonny.

My guess was that it was Sonny. I was right. He flew up the stairs and took me in his arms the moment he came through the door—like the old poster from *Gone With The Wind*. My, he was happy, not to mention wild and almost incoherent.

"Revenge is sweet, isn't it? Sweeter than wine!"

Finally he calmed down and sat on the sofa.

"Mei has been talking," Sonny explained, "And while he hasn't given us Wu yet, he's given us a lot. Interpol has rolled up the whole damned overseas operation—the poachers, the preparers, the shippers, everyone."

"That's wonderful, Sonny." It had obviously been a productive week for him and the NYPD.

"We don't have the head of the snake yet. We don't have Wu yet. But we'll get him. . . . I need some juice, Alice. Do you have any apple juice?"

I brought him a glass of cranapple juice. He drank it greedily and half choked. I took the glass away from him.

"And all those clowns at RETRO who used to say I made detective only because I speak Chinese . . . who used to say I couldn't pull my weight . . . they're all eating crow. Publicly. This is turning out to be the biggest case RETRO has cleared in years. And it's all mine!"

I didn't know what to say. I was happy for Sonny's success, but I was confused. He seemed to be giving me absolutely no credit, even in his own mind. Powered rhino horn at five hundred dollars per ounce seemed to have induced memory loss when it came to a restaurant shooting, the murder of a waitress, and the disappearance of a lovely red tabby.

He closed his eyes and flung his arms expansively over the back of the sofa. He was quiet, gathering his strength.

Pancho then zoomed into the room, for some reason took a swipe at one of Sonny's shoes, missed, and zoomed off to the windowsill.

Bushy watched without comment. I felt an enormous proprietary tenderness for all three of my felines.

Then Sonny opened his eyes. "The best is yet to come, Alice," he said, laughing again. "RETRO has rented a suite of rooms at the Gramercy Park

Hotel for six o'clock this evening. And they're filling the rooms with champagne and goodies. And toasting *me*! A victory party for none other than Emerson 'Sonny' Hoving, new star of the NYPD. And you, madam, are one of the guests of honor."

"You deserve a victory party," I said.

"I surely do," he agreed.

I wondered how much my old RETRO friend Rothwax knew about my involvement in the case and my affair with Sonny.

"But right now I need a favor, Alice," Sonny said.

"Sure."

He held up a small satchel that I hadn't even noticed when he'd entered my apartment. It was the kind old men carry to gyms.

"The property clerk has released Nancy Han's stuff. Mostly the clothes she was wearing that night and some little things she had in her locker at the restaurant." He unzipped the bag and showed me. It was very sad.

"I called Mrs. Han. She lives in those Gold Street projects just before you get to the South Street Seaport. She'll be home from work at four-thirty this afternoon. I thought maybe you could do me a favor and bring them to her, then go straight up to the party at the Gramercy Park Hotel. I have a lot of things to do, Alice. I just don't have time to deliver it." He zipped up the bag and patted it, waiting for my answer.

Was it simply that Sonny didn't have the heart to deliver the bag . . . that delivering a dead daughter's work clothes to a mother was just too much for him? Regardless, I agreed to do it. What did it matter why?

Sonny babbled on about RETRO and the party, about Rothwax, about the powered rhino horn, and then he ran out as quickly as he had run in, leaving the small bag on the floor.

I arrived in front of Mrs. Han's apartment door at twenty to five that afternoon. I had already dressed for Sonny's party. I carried the bag gingerly, as if it contained a bomb. The apartment was in one of those very well-maintained middle-class projects that were built in the 1950s and '60s.

Mrs. Han answered the bell on the first ring. It was obvious she was expecting the bag, and it was also obvious she had just come home from work. Looking past her through the doorway I could see the just-collected but unopened mail on a table.

Mrs. Han, who looked uncomfortably like her murdered daughter, did not ask me if I was a police officer. She very politely ushered me in and led me to a high-back chair. I sat down. She sat down opposite me in a twin of the chair I was seated on. She was very well dressed.

"These then, are the clothes Nancy was wearing when she was murdered," Mrs. Han said softly. I couldn't tell whether it was a question or a statement.

I nodded, zipped open the bag, and placed it on the floor in front of Mrs. Han. She stared at it and seemed about to look through the contents . . . when, suddenly, a flash of such intense anguish crossed her face that I thought she would collapse. I started out of my chair toward the poor woman, but she halted me with a gesture and fought to gain control over her emotions.

"I am . . . making . . . some tea," she said haltingly. "May I get you some?" I nodded. Mrs. Han left the room and returned a few minutes later with two cups. The tea was very strong and very hot. I cradled the cup in the palms of my hands.

"It is very hard to believe my daughter is truly dead," Mrs. Han said, almost in a whisper. "I still set the alarm for her each morning so that she gets up in time for her classes."

Then she placed her teacup on an adjoining table and bent over to bring the small satchel up to her lap.

At that moment, a cat sauntered into the room and walked between our two chairs.

Mrs. Han ignored the cat. I caught my breath.

It was a large red tabby, and it nonchalantly lay down five feet from Mrs. Han's chair.

Was I dreaming? What madness was this?

The cat who had just sauntered by was *Millie*!

I kept staring at the cat while Mrs. Han went through her daughter's belongings. It *was* Millie! It was—beyond a shadow of a doubt—the kitchen cat from Dan Wu's restaurant! A surge of joy. She was safe and well! Then a larger surge of confusion. What on earth was Millie doing in Mrs. Han's apartment?

Forcing the growing excitement out of my voice, I asked Mrs. Han quietly, "Have you had that cat a long time?"

Mrs. Han looked at me, then at the cat. She smiled. "Oh, not long at all. She's a lovely cat, isn't she? It is a very strange thing. About three days after Nancy was murdered, an old man came to my door, assisted by a young man. They were both Chinese. The old man offered his condolences and gave me the cat, saying it would help me in these sad times. I didn't know who they were. I was so astonished that I couldn't even respond.

They left immediately. . . . She paused and stared at Millie. "But the old man was right. She *has* been a great comfort to me."

She shook her head. "It was all so strange. It all happened so fast."

"Did the old man tell you his name?"

"He did, but I don't remember it."

"Do you remember anything else about them? It is important for you to remember, Mrs. Han. It may help us find out who murdered your daughter."

Mrs. Han's eyes opened wide in shock and perplexity; no doubt she was thinking that the gentle old man who had visited her couldn't possibly have had anything to do with her daughter's death. She zippered shut the small satchel. "I remember looking out my window after they left. I saw them both climb into a very old pickup truck. Painted green. There was a sign on the side of the truck . . . it read something like 'Good Taste Farm.' I remember there were the initials N.J. after the name—for New Jersey, I suppose. And there was a village or a town, also. Something like Deedsboro or Swaleboro."

Millie was now sidling against Mrs. Han's leg and Mrs. Han responded by scratching the cat gently between the ears.

"It's hard for me to remember things lately . . . very hard." She picked Millie up and hugged her. Then she burst out: "Wait! Yes! I remember the old man's name. Mr. Shih. That's it. Mr. Shih."

"Was his full name Ch'in Shih?" I asked, the name popping out of my consciousness before I could even identify it.

"I don't know his full name," Mrs. Han said.

But suddenly *I* knew the name Ch'in Shih. In

Dan Wu's cookbook, *Five Flavors,* in the chapter on soup, the author mentions his indebtedness to one Ch'in Shih. But who was he?

"Would you like more tea?" Mrs. Han asked.

"I am sorry, but I can't stay any longer." We both stood up and said good-bye, sadly. I wanted very much to kiss Millie, but all I did was shake one paw. She yawned.

Back on the street, I was bewildered. Everything was coming in a rush. Thank God Millie was okay, but it was obvious I had been right all along—she had been taken from the restaurant the night of the shooting.

A whole new scenario was beginning to form in my head. The kidnapped Millie. The old Chinese man. The cookbook. The Chinese character drawn on the wall. Harmony.

I started to walk uptown. First things first. I had to go to the RETRO party for Sonny. More important, I had to speak to Sonny, fast.

20

The RETRO party was not in a suite of rooms as Sonny had claimed; it was in a small space on the second floor of the hotel, half closed-in by portable screens. I should have expected as much, since those kinds of parties are paid for by voluntary contributions and therefore, always a bit tacky.

When I arrived it was close to seven P.M. and the party was in full gear. It was crowded, very crowded, and loud, and the smoke was thick. A long table was covered with platters of food, the cellophane pulled back. A small table had bottles of champagne and whiskey and soft drinks, and under the table were several tubs of bottled beer in ice.

I spotted Detective Rothwax first—he was behind the table dispensing drinks. He saw me, waved, and grinned. I knew immediately from the construct of his grin that he was aware Sonny and I were, or had been, lovers.

Two quasi-intoxicated cops drifted past. They stopped and looked me over lasciviously. One said, "Well, the stripper is here. Where's the chop suey?" I turned away from those leering idiots. Poor Sonny. He probably had to hear bad chop suey and won ton soup jokes every day of his professional life.

Then I saw Sonny, dressed in his usual disreputable style. He was standing in the corner, in front of a screen, smiling broadly at nothing in particular, a glass of champagne in his hand. Sonny didn't drink, usually, but he was obviously imbibing now. I stayed back and watched, gathering my thoughts. From time to time various people approached him and offered their congratulations. He didn't speak, just smiled and returned the handshake heartily. It was obvious he was relishing his moment of triumph.

I stared back toward Rothwax, but he had vanished from his bartending chores. I looked carefully around. There were only one or two other faces I remembered from my short tenure at RETRO.

Then Sonny spotted me and waved. I quickly walked over to him.

"It's about time you arrived, about time!" he said in mock anger. I kissed him on the cheek. The champagne had given his face a lovely glow.

I asked him in a low voice, "Can we go somewhere else for a few minutes? I have to talk to you."

"Talk here. We're among friends."

He put his hand on my shoulder in a manner that I didn't like . . . as if he were showing his friends that he owned this tall woman.

"Sonny, I don't think the shooting in the restaurant had anything to do with the smuggling operation."

He grinned. "Is that so?"

"And I think Wu was telling the truth about trying to stop his partner's criminal enterprise."

"This is getting even funnier, Alice," he said, rocking back on his heels and drinking more champagne.

"And I'm almost sure Dan Wu knows who shot up the restaurant and why—and it has nothing to do with rhino horn."

The look of amused superiority left his face. "Are you serious about this? Do you really expect me to believe all that?"

Then he grabbed me harshly by the arm and whispered in an ugly tone, "I'm beginning to see what you want from me, Alice. You want me to stay your little boy. You want me to be your lap-dog. Is that it? You can't stand the fact that I won a great victory . . . that I stood alone."

I shook off his hurtful grip.

"Listen to me, Sonny. I found Millie. I found the cat. She was taken from the restaurant that night. She was kidnapped."

He laughed so loudly and so cruelly that many eyes in the party began to focus on us.

"So that's it, huh, Alice? Your great investigative leap? The cat was kidnapped." He then turned to the partyers, many of whom had turned to gawk, and repeated the last line louder and with a terrible sarcasm.

"The cat was kidnapped!" Then Sonny spotted Rothwax and he shouted at him, "You *told* me she was crazy! But I didn't believe you. You *told* me she's a crazy Cat Woman. And I didn't believe a word."

"You're shouting, Sonny, keep your voice down."

"Don't tell me what to do!" he screamed at me.

"I may be a crazy Cat Woman, but you're pathetic. Your case is even more pathetic. I told you the truth."

"Shut up!"

"You're acting like a five-year-old."

"Bitch!" he screamed at me. He seemed to have lost every last shred of sense, and dignity. The alcohol had taken over, along with a lot of other feelings I had never known he had. I turned away from him and started to walk away.

He grabbed my arm and spun me around. "Bitch! Stupid, manipulative, soul-sucking bitch!" he screamed. Then he flung what was left in his champagne glass into my face.

I have never felt such rage, hurt, and shame in my entire life.

Oh, I realized what he was going through. This party was his entrance into RETRO and all it stood for. His breaking of the case was his initiation into the The Club. Now he was no longer the weird Eurasian outsider. Now he was one of the guys. And I had spoiled all of that. Yes, I understood. But I could not forgive.

I walked out of that party and that hotel very slowly, because weakness seemed to be flowing through my limbs and I was afraid I would collapse.

I didn't collapse. I got home with my body in one piece, and my soul shattered.

21

The rage lasted twenty-four hours, the pain forty-eight. But after seventy-two, the shame was still alive and well. Shame that I had fallen in love with Sonny Hoving. Shame that I had been so foolishly in love I could not see what had to happen sooner or later. Shame at a thousand things. Deep, humiliating shame that kept me silent in a darkened apartment.

Of course, all during those first three days after the debacle at the party, Sonny kept calling to apologize. I hung up and finally didn't answer at all. He tried ringing the downstairs buzzer. He tried sending flowers by messenger. He tried everything, but all I wanted was to be left alone. I did not wish to see him or to speak to him. I wanted, above all, to be rid of him and all memories of him. I wanted to be rid of the promise of love.

At the end of the fourth day I emerged from my apartment. A piece of folded white paper was Scotch-taped onto my mailbox. I was about to rip it to pieces, thinking it was from Sonny, when it fell open by itself and I saw Tony Basillio's handwriting:

Have been trying to contact you for three days. Back in Pickwick Arms. Call. Come. T.

Yes, I needed a friend. I forgot about the shopping I had planned and took a cab to his hotel. I called from the lobby and he answered on the first ring and told me to come up.

Tony was waiting for me at the elevator, and he hit me with a furious barrage: "What the hell is going on with you? You don't answer phones or doorbells. You don't write. You just vanish. I know you're in love, but—"

I held up my hand for him to stop. He shut up, no doubt having finally seen my pallor.

Then he asked, with concern, "What's the matter with you, Swede?" He took my arm and led me to his room as if I were an invalid.

"It's over," I said wearily as soon as I had sat down on the single overstuffed chair in his room. "It's all over."

"I'm sorry," he replied.

His hair was longer than ever. And he looked like he hadn't shaved in days. "I didn't mean to be cruel, Tony. I shouldn't have told you at all. I don't know why I told you over the phone. I am so ashamed of the way—" He held up his hand to tell me no apology was necessary.

"I'm pathetic," I said bitterly.

"No more than me."

"Oh yes, Tony. You don't know the half of it."

"But I fall in love every six weeks," he replied jauntily.

"That's news to me," I said, laughing for the first time in days.

"We should get drunk together, Alice Nestleton. I'm going to be around for about a week."

"Yes, we should. But—"

"But what?" he interrupted, producing a small mint wrapped in silver foil. I took the piece of candy, unwrapped it, but then had no desire to taste it at all. He shrugged, retrieved it, and popped it into his mouth.

I started to cry.

"It'll take a while, but you'll get over it," he said.

"There's more involved than an affair," I replied.

"What can be more than an affair?"

"A murder."

"Whose murder?"

Then I told him everything, starting with the dinner engagement with the film producer in Dan Wu's restaurant. I described the shooting. Millie. How I met Sonny. How I met Dan Wu and Jack Pallister. How I led Sonny to Dr. Mei and the powdered rhino horn. The old man who delivered the kitchen cat to Mrs. Han. Everything. It was a very long story and Tony listened in silence, grimacing only when I recounted what happened at the RETRO party after I had found Millie.

When I was finished, he said, "You've been busy. And here I thought all you were doing was making love."

"Can you bring me some water, Tony?"

He brought me a glass of cold water from the bathroom sink, then studied me as I drank. "You look like you're not finished with this affair," he noted.

"Oh, please."

"No, I mean you look like you want to continue the investigation."

"I'm tired. I'm heartsick. But yes, you're right."

"Is it revenge?"

"Revenge?"

"Yes, your way of getting back at Sonny; showing him you were right all along."

"Maybe a little of that. But there's a great deal more. There's a dead girl, Tony. And a bizarre, exasperating man who I want to . . ." I couldn't find the right word to describe my need to unravel the mystery of Dan Wu, so I settled for "disrobe."

Tony found that very funny. Then he said, "Well, as I said, you have me for a week. If you need me."

"I need you, Tony."

Refreshed by the thought of being able to continue, happy that Tony had so quickly forgiven me my indiscretion, I sketched out for him what Mrs. Han had remembered about the old man Ch'in Shih.

When I got to her attempt to recall the village in New Jersey that had been written on the side of the old pickup truck, Tony guffawed.

"What's so funny?"

"A private joke. Listen, what's my usual nickname for you?"

"Swede, I suppose."

"Right. And that's the village your Mrs. Han couldn't piece together. The Good Taste Farm is in *Swedesboro*, New Jersey."

"How can you be sure?"

"It makes sense. It's close to Mrs. Han's 'Deedsboro' or 'Swalesboro' and I happen to know that Swedesboro is a farming area in South Jersey that has become home to a lot of Chinese, Korean, and Vietnamese farmers who truck their vegetables into the Asian restaurants in New York, Philadelphia, and Washington."

"Can you take me there?"

"When?"

"Now. This afternoon. This evening. Tomorrow morning. Anytime."

"Tomorrow morning it shall be," Tony replied, then collapsed on the floor and stretched out all his limbs. It didn't strike me as peculiar at all. One never knew what he would do. Unlike me, of course, a.k.a. the rock of Gibraltar. Ha!

So that explains why, the next morning, Tony Basillio and I were once again sharing a rented car. He was driving. It was a long, silent trip. My psychic wounds were still apparent. His concern for my wounds inhibited his usual bantering.

We drove almost the entire length of the New Jersey Turnpike and then turned west. Yes, there was a town called Swedesboro, and yes, it was a farming community. It was in a part of New Jersey that I never knew existed; a part where one could easily get stuck on a country road behind three tractors motoring happily along at their snail's pace.

We ate lunch in town—grilled cheese sandwiches. The first person we asked—a private garbage center—knew exactly where The Good Taste farm was—about eight miles outside of town. He gave us exact directions.

A dirt road branched off from the county road and took us to the farm. It was pitted with some of the meanest potholes I've ever been jounced by, and it ended abruptly. About fifty feet from the end stood a lovely, small, freshly painted white-frame house.

Tony and I got out of the car and stood there in the silence of a lovely early afternoon. Behind the farmhouse were a few sheds, perhaps housing goats or hogs or chickens. Radiating out from a point just past the sheds were the fields. Ah, they were a beautiful sight. The terrain was slightly hilly, and the crops seemed to roll over the land. The farm was planted in quarter-acre sections. There were cabbages and tomatoes and peppers and different kinds of radishes and onions. The late spring air was heavy with their growing. One could hear them.

"I don't see anyone," Tony said nervously.

Not only didn't we see anyone, we saw no implements on the ground—no old barrels or hoses or tractor parts or car tires. And that was very odd, very odd indeed. My grandmother was a fastidious woman, but even her dairy farm was littered with abandoned tools and machines of all kinds. Farms always have trouble with disposal. It's part of their charm and their frugality. But not true, apparently, of The Good Taste Farm.

"Are you lost?"

The voice startled us. We had already approached the house, and the voice came from behind us. We turned.

A young Asian man stood not more than ten feet from us, a coil of irrigation hosing around his shoulder. He was dressed in jeans and boots, and naked from the waist up. He was very thin.

"Are you lost?" he repeated.

I stared wide-eyed at the young man. Yes, he was Chinese. Was this the young man who had accompanied the old man to Mrs. Han?

Another thought chilled me. Was this one of the young men who had shot up the restaurant? He was of that age. And his face seemed vaguely familiar. But I couldn't be sure. I would have to see him in different clothes.

"We're looking for Mr. Ch'in Shih," I finally announced.

"I am afraid he is ill. He cannot speak to anyone now," the young man explained politely.

"It will only take a moment. It's very important."

"I am afraid he cannot speak to anyone."

"Look!" Tony said suddenly, pointing to a tilled field running parallel to the far side of the white house.

An old man was standing there, about twenty rows in. He was wearing a large straw hat against the sun, a woman's hat, much like the one I had used in following Jack Pallister. He also wore a long body shirt with a leather belt around his middle. Even from that distance I could see he was a very old man and he was standing absolutely still, as if in contemplation. His head was inclined away, not looking in our direction.

"Is that Mr. Ch'in Shih?" I blurted out to the young man.

"No."

"Then who is it?"

"I don't know. Perhaps a scarecrow. Perhaps a cousin of Ch'in Shih. I think now you had better leave."

For the first time there was a threat in his voice. Tony and I walked back to the car. I called out to the young man, "Please tell Mr. Ch'in Shih that I wished to talk to him about Dan Wu's kitchen cat."

The young man bowed.

I was about to climb into my seat when three tiny shapes darted out from under the car. Kittens! Plump, wild, lovely little farm kittens, jumping and tumbling after one another.

Tony laughed. "Grab one, Alice. That's what

you need— another cat in your apartment. Bushy and Pancho are getting bored with each other."

I didn't laugh. Two of the three bounding kittens were a very distinct type—red tabby! Were these kittens Millie's nieces and nephews? Grandchildren? I looked around, confused . . . at the young man waiting for us to leave . . . at the old man standing in the field, motionless. Was this place Millie's original home?

Then we both climbed into the car and drove off the property. Tony pulled the car to the side of the road about a quarter-mile from The Good Taste Farm.

"Strange, unfriendly people," he said.

When I didn't respond, he asked, "What do we do now? Do you want to go back later?"

"I don't know. I don't know what to do."

"Why wouldn't that old man even listen to you?"

"I don't know."

I leaned back against the seat and closed my eyes. The visit had exhausted me. The young man had frightened me. The kittens and the old man had confused me.

Tony started to tap on the wheel with his fingers.

"We can drive back to town and start again tomorrow, Swede. Or we can try our luck at the farm again this evening. Or we can take a motel room and stay down here and explore the town and try and find out more about The Good Taste Farm. There are a lot of things we can do." He kept tapping the wheel as he outlined the options.

But Tony was wrong. I really didn't have any more options at all. Oh, I could go through the motions. But it would be a mime show. Even if I had been able to meet with Ch'in Shih, I knew in my heart it would have been futile.

I was missing something. I was not plugged in. I was not connected to their world.

I knew that the whole conspiracy was right out in the open . . . that I had every one of the pieces . . . but I simply couldn't put the whole thing together because the puzzles were different.

It was that simple. I needed just one Rosetta stone with a translation. That's all I needed. That would cause all the facades to crumble.

"What I need, Tony, is an orientalist. That's what I have to do next. Find one . . . and talk to one."

"Where do you find one? In the Yellow Pages?"

"I don't know."

"Of course," Tony said, laughing hugely, "I can always take you to Reuben Tarnapol."

The mention of that name evoked a memory. A moody, long-haired actor and playwright who said little and always paced; a man who seemed to be permanently afflicted with an agitated depression; a very strange individual who, when he did talk, would draw his words from Hesse's novel *Steppenwolf* or the *I Ching*.

"That's a real name form the past," I noted, smiling sadly.

"Yes it is," Tony affirmed, "from when we both were young and beautiful and unstoppable."

"What happened to him? I remember someone telling me that he went to Ceylon and became a Buddhist monk."

"He did that. And he did a lot of other things after Ceylon. India and Nepal and Tibet and Hong Kong. Buddhism, Taoism, kung fu. Who knows what else?"

"Have you seen him recently? I mean, is he alive and well?"

"He called me a couple of months ago. Sure, he's alive. I don't know how well he is . . . I mean in the head. Anyway, he bought a small bed and breakfast place in Cape May, at the southern tip of the Jersey shore. The only thing he does now is bird-watching. With a vengeance. That's why he's living there. It's a bird-watcher's paradise. On the migration routes."

"Do you think he would help me?" I asked.

"I'm sure he'd be willing. I mean, I don't know what kind of information you're looking for. But if it's about the mystical, the strange . . . with an oriental tinge . . . he's your man."

"Cape May is on the other side of the state," I noted.

"A few hours. We can stay with him when we get there. All you have to do is call your neighbor to feed your cats."

I sat in silence and pondered. I knew Cap May: a lovely little seaside town, filled with Victorian gingerbread houses. I had performed there in the mid-1980s, in one of the many art festivals the town was always sponsoring to bring in some tourists beyond the usual bird-watchers and sunbathers.

"Reuben Tarnapol." I repeated the name slowly. Why not? What did I have to lose? My head was full of sputtering intuitions and frayed connections. All I needed was one spark to light them all, to fuse them. Why shouldn't an old acting acquaintance, obsessed with things Chinese, provide that spark? Why indeed?

"Let's go, Tony," I said.

22

It was a miserable trip across the state of New Jersey to Cape May—as usual, Tony refused to follow any map's instructions. If a road on a map looked like the straightest line between two points, he immediately distrusted it and searched out an alternate route.

So it was early evening when we finally did arrive. The place hadn't changed. Along the beachfront were the large hotels and motels, many of them boarded up, relics of an era long past. But the bustling village mall—several streets on which no vehicles were allowed—still had its many upscale stores and restaurants, including a gift shop just for bird-watchers.

All the houses in Cape May seemed to have been freshly painted for the coming summer season, vibrant blues and whites and pinks and greens. Half the houses seemed to have BED & BREAKFAST signs, and many of the larger ones had enclosed porches.

Once inside Cape May, Tony got lost again. "The name of the place is The Softly Falcon Inn," he muttered, "and it's supposed to be two blocks from the Visitors' Center. We just passed the Center. Where's the Inn?"

"What kind of name is that, Tony? The 'Softly Falcon' Inn? It makes no sense."

"Sounds good to me," he replied.

Finally Tony located it, and pulled the car in front. It was probably the only B & B in Cape May that hadn't been painted. In fact, it looked downright dilapidated. No wonder—beneath a sign reading THE SOFTLY FALCON INN/BED & BREAKFAST was another in red letters that proclaimed the place CLOSED.

"Maybe he moved," I suggested.

"He's here," Tony said, "I sense him." We climbed out of the car and up the porch steps of The Softly Falcon Inn.

There was a huge brass knob. Tony slammed it thrice. A man opened the door, and the moment he saw us his face broke out in a wide smile.

Was *this* Reuben Tarnapol? How could it be? That Reuben had had long hair and a smooth face. This one was bald with a beard. That Reuben was thin. This Reuben was portly.

But it *was* Reuben Tarnapol twenty years later, and he was very happy to see me again. He led us inside.

"I stopped renting out rooms a couple of months ago," he explained. "Why bother? I don't need the money."

The downstairs area consisted of a sitting room, a large dining room, and a kitchen with one of those black industrial stoves. Reuben led us through the kitchen and into a storeroom area, which seemed to be the only place on that level that was lived in. There were several easy chairs, a small refrigerator, and three television sets. Along the walls were shovels and rakes and other tools.

We sat down. Tony asked, "Why three television sets?"

"For my three VCRs," Reuben said. Then he picked up three videotapes, slammed them into the VCRs, and turned them all on at once.

Each one showed birds in flight.

"Beautiful, aren't they? I shot these all last fall, using the birding platforms in the state park." Reuben began to excitedly describe what was coming up next on each tape. I could see several video cameras stacked along one wall.

"Look at that . . . there," he said, pointing to one of the screens on which two hawks flew in tandem, their wings beating powerfully and concurrently against the wind currents.

As suddenly as he had put the tapes on, he turned them off. "You people must be hungry and thirsty," he said. He opened the refrigerator and took out the remaining half of a large Boston Cream Pie. He laid it out in front of us on a small folding table with napkins and plastic spoons, then brought two bottles of Italian white wine. He opened them and poured out three paper cups full.

Sitting down expansively, he said, "God, I hate theater people." Then he started to laugh uproariously at his own joke, whatever it was. Tony gave me a look signifying that he thought Reuben Tarnapol was no longer playing with a full deck, to use a "Tonyism."

"It has been a long time," Reuben said sadly, "and we have all ended up so strangely."

This conversation, if you could call it that, was making Tony nervous. "Is that all you do now, Reuben? Videotape birds in flight?"

"Well," Reuben said, helping himself to a spoonful of the cream pie, "I also write about birds." A speck of pie landed on his denim shirt. He stared at it, then ignored it.

"My project is going quite well, in fact."

"What project?" Tony asked.

"I am going to create the first bird-identification guide based on the new evidence."

"What evidence?" I asked.

"That birds are the sole surviving ancestors of the dinosaurs."

"But how does that affect the way one identifies a bird?" I asked. "I mean, a blue jay is still a blue jay."

"You're right. It doesn't. As the Zen Buddhists say: 'Before you are enlightened, mountains are mountains and rivers are rivers. After you are enlightened, mountains are mountains and rivers are rivers.'"

"So why write new bird books?" Tony pressed on.

"No, not *new* bird books per se. A new *kind* of bird book, so that the bird-watcher, each time he consults his book, is made aware that standing behind that tiny bird, in time and space, is that enormously tragic, complex, and beautiful race of beings called the dinosaurs."

We both were beginning to get a bit uncomfortable. Neither of us had ever heard dinosaurs described in such a fashion.

But the discomfort diminished very quickly, for a moment later Reuben began to talk about the old days. About what he remembered of theater people and places and productions. About the world of the acting student in Manhattan in the early 1970s. About women he had been in love with, and teachers he had despised. About the food and the despair and the joy and the apartments and the parties and the corrosive, doomed freedom of it all. And after each excavation in the care of memory he would look at either Tony or me and say, "Do you remember her?" Or, "Remember that?" Or, "How sad it was!"

By the time Reuben finally returned to the present, it was pitch-dark outside. Tony had repeatedly dozed off. The wine was gone. The Boston Cream Pie was *long* gone. There seemed to be nothing further to say or remember.

It was time for me to take center stage.

"Reuben! I came here with Tony because I need your help in a murder investigation."

"And to think I thought you came here," he said slyly, "to go back in time . . . to sit again in a seedy Manhattan bar, holding hands, talking about something real—the theater."

"Same old Reuben," Tony said, emerging from his doze. "His reality was always different."

"Of course it's different from yours," Reuben replied happily, "because you are from the West and I am from the East. And we both know where the sun rises."

"That's exactly it," I interjected. "That's why I need your help."

"You have my help."

"Tell him the whole crazy story," Tony suggested.

No, I couldn't. I didn't want to. It was too wearisome. I would get right to the point.

"Have you ever heard of Dan Wu?"

"No. Wait . . . yes . . . you mean the television chef."

"Exactly. Dan Wu, the sometime television chef and restaurateur. Now on the face of it this man is rational, ambitious, creative, Western-dressed, English-speaking . . . and above all, comprehensible."

"Is he a suspect in the murder?"

"I don't know yet. At first I believed in his reality, if you know what I mean. I believed he was exactly as he looked, spoke, acted. But then something happened."

"What?"

"I had a five-minute conversation alone with him, a conversation about a cat, and I realized that he's not at all as he appears. And that's where I'm stuck."

"What did he say?"

"First of all, when I described seeing a cat perched high on kitchen shelving in his restaurant, he wondered whether it wasn't a cat looking at the moon."

The moment I had finished uttering those words Reuben burst out of his chair and threw himself into a series of body movements so bizarre that Tony and I stared at each other in total perplexity.

He ended them as quickly as he had begun them, bowed, and sat back down, grinning.

I didn't know what to say.

"That, Alice Nestleton," Reuben explained, "is a *Cat Looking at the Moon.* It is part of the Marrow-Washing Classic—a very ancient series of stretching exercises for spiritual and physical health. Supposedly the exercises were invented by the first Buddhist patriarch in China, but the Taoists made them famous in their monasteries. Individual exercises have all kinds of strange names like Clutching Eagle and Fisherman Rows the Boat."

His insights both excited and unnerved me.

"What else?" he asked.

Now I was eager to go on. "When I persisted in questioning him about the kitchen cat, he said a very strange thing. He said there was no cat in his kitchen. What I had seen was a dragon. And he seemed quite serious about it."

Reuben didn't answer for a while. He stared at Tony and me, then at the pie stain on his shirt.

Finally he said, "Well, I imagine he was serious. The most powerful hexagram in the *I Ching* is the Khien hexagram. It incorporates both Yin and Yang. The real power of this hexagram in the science of divination lies in the fact that a dragon is lurking within it. The true practitioner of *I Ching* can bring this dragon up from the depths in all its awesome strength."

I pressed on, more and more engrossed. "And then Dan Wu denied that there was any cat or any dragon or any animal of any kind in his kitchen. He said that I spent too much time traveling back and forth, in and out, to find the truth. He said I should stay at home. He said that one could discover the truth of all things without moving at all."

Reuben nodded his head vigorously up and down. "That's pure Lao-tzu, the great philosopher who wrote the *Tao Te Ching*. In English it's called *The Doctrine of the Power of the Way*. It's the most famous and influential Chinese philosophical work ever written. He was, essentially, the founder of Taoism. He lived around 500 B.C."

"But you make Dan Wu sound like a holy man," I blurted out.

"If the shoe fits . . ." Reuben mused. "And besides, you told me you knew he was not what he appeared. He was not the quintessential celebrity chef."

"Tell him about the old man, Chan Shu," Tony urged.

"His name is Ch'in Shih," I corrected Tony. Then I told Reuben about the old man; about how

Dan Wu had eulogized him cryptically in his cookbook; how the old man had paid a condolence call on the murder victim's mother and given her the cat that had been taken during the shooting; how we had journeyed to his little farm but been denied access to him; and about the strangeness of his appearance.

Reuben shrugged, then said, "Maybe the old man was Dan Wu's teacher."

"Teacher of what?"

"I don't know. Maybe he taught Wu how to cook. Maybe he's Wu's guru. Maybe the old man is a Taoist priest."

Tony laughed. "Are you kidding? He has a vest-pocket farm in South Jersey and grows cabbages. He's a damned truck farmer. How could he be a Taoist priest?"

"You obviously don't understand Taoism, Tony," Reuben chastised, but kindly. "Many Taoist priests left the monastery and assumed a wandering life. As beggars. As shoemakers. As herders. And many settled down and became farmers. That is the essence of Taoism: that it doesn't matter what you do or who you are. It is all the same. One should not strive or fight against fate. If one wants to walk—by all means walk. If one ends up farming—by all means farm. It is the hallowed 'middle way.' Fat people should eat less—yes. But they should not fast. Skinny people should eat more—yes. But they should not gorge. All extremes must be avoided. Only in the 'middle way' is there harmony. Take a traditional Chinese meal, for example. The more different kinds of food the better. The more varied the dishes, the more harmony. But never one food in excess."

"You are exhausting me with your Oriental wisdom," Tony said. "How about showing me the 'middle way' to bed."

Yes, it was late. Reuben led us upstairs, where we had the pick of seven possible bedrooms.

I closed the door of the room of my choice and sat on the edge of the bed.

There were beads of cold sweat on my forehead, but they weren't there because I had no change of clothes and no toilet articles or because I was exhausted.

They were there because Reuben's explanation of the "middle way" had jiggled the last piece into place for me.

I knew what had happened! I understood what had transpired, and why!

But along with understanding came the absolute surety that no one—not Rothwax, not Sonny, not Tony—would believe me. Because what had happened was very strange . . . the motives alien . . . the cover-up incomprehensible.

Yes, everything had become clear. But now I had to prove it.

I sat there and wondered: How does one prove the outlandish? How does one prove that black may be white? Green, purple? East, West? How does one prove that an out-of-work actor can be a genius at least for one day?

I must have fretted for an hour over the injustice of it all—the clock said it was one-twenty in the morning—and then I started to laugh.

I fully realized why I was laughing. Because all I needed to resolve the Dan Wu case, if one could call it that, was on the floor below. Yes, there was a kitchen and a video camera down there. What else did I truly need?

And then I slept the sleep of the just.

23

"Where's Reuben?" I asked.

Tony didn't reply to my question. He said: "Swede, you should break up a love affair once a month. I don't ever remember you sleeping so late in the morning. It's good for you. You came down those stairs like an ingenue."

Tony was using the enormous restaurant range in the large kitchen to boil some water for instant coffee. The poor little pot looked lost. On the table were cups with the instant coffee spooned out, waiting for the water to boil, and a stale loaf of rye bread in cellophane. Waiting beside the bread was a plate, and on the plate was a forlorn slab of what may have been scallion cream cheese. It's for the best, I thought, that Reuben doesn't rent rooms anymore.

"Where's Reuben?" I repeated my question.

"Out shooting birds with his video cameras. He must have left the house around six o'clock."

"Do you think, Tony, that Reuben will let us use his house?"

"For what, illicit purposes? Are you making a pass at me, Swede?"

He poured the hot water into my cup. Seconds later we heard the front door open and Reuben came sauntering in, his video cameras on his shoulder and in his hands several containers of coffee and fresh donuts for us. He laid them out on the long kitchen table.

"Too foggy out," he said disgustedly, and sat down heavily. Then he brightened. "If you want to do exercises, I can show you all of the ones in the Marrow-Washing Classic."

"I think I'll pass," I said. I broke a donut in half and tasted it. Very fresh.

"If it wasn't for the morning fogs, this place would be paradise," Reuben said.

I sipped the fresh container of coffee. Reuben had put too much sugar in . . . *and* there was milk in it. But I managed to cope.

It was time to set everything into motion.

"Would you let me use your kitchen for a cooking class?" I asked him.

He stared at me wide-eyed, then at Tony. Tony in turn asked, "Are you serious?"

"Quite serious."

"A new hobby, Swede?"

"No, I'm not going to be conducting the class, Tony. Dan Wu is."

"Did you ask him?"

"No. But he will."

"Sure. A world-class, millionaire chef, who may or may not be a figure in Asian organized crime, is going to come to Cape May, to Reuben's kitchen, and teach locals how to use a wok."

I ignored him. I would have to keep Tony in the dark, the same as Reuben. I needed Tony and trusted him, but I just couldn't handle the constant sarcasm and questioning that would come my way if I revealed what I was up to.

"It will only be a one-day course, Reuben. You know, one of those all-day seminars—about eight hours. Maybe eight to ten students, each one paying two hundred dollars or so for the privilege. And of course, you'll get a percentage."

Reuben looked confused. "I really don't need the money, Alice. I just don't know."

"Well, Reuben, if you don't need the money, do it for me, for old times' sake."

"But you told me you were trying to solve a murder involving this Dan Wu. What does this cooking class have to do with anything?" Reuben asked.

"It's just something I've always wanted to do," I lied. "And it gives me a chance to get closer to Dan Wu." Tony was beginning to look at me through narrowed eyes. "Look, Reuben," I continued, "you won't be involved. Today's Wednesday, right? Tony and I will leave today. We'll drive back down next Tuesday morning, very early. The students for the class will be registering that day, and I'll answer all the phones. The next day will be the class, and then it's all over. I'll clean up."

Reuben sighed mightily and then said, "Okay. Why not?"

"There's one other favor I need to ask of you, Reuben. Could you videotape it for me?"

"You mean the whole eight-hour class?"

"Yes. But not the way you think. I want it cinema verité. I don't want the students to know they're being taped. I thought maybe you could hook up some video cameras in the storeroom. Maybe behind a curtain."

The idea caught Reuben's fancy. It was obviously the kind of challenge he relished.

He said happily, "It can be done. Yes, sure. I can set up about four cameras, timed to go on one after another every forty-five minutes or so and then shut off. Two will always be working in tandem, covering different quadrants of the kitchen. Yes, it can be done. It's an interesting problem. We won't catch everything, but we'll catch a lot. Sure."

"I assume, Alice," Tony said wryly, "that you're going to reimburse Reuben for the videotape . . . or at the very least give him a piece of the action when this classic gets picked up by PBS."

I ignored him. "One other thing, Reuben. Would you mind if Dan Wu brought his cat?"

"I like cats," Reuben said.

Tony interjected again, "I thought you told me his cat, Millie, was kidnapped from the restaurant and given to Mrs. Han."

"That was his kitchen cat, from the restaurant. I'm talking about Dan Wu's house cat," I lied again.

"Do you want me to buy some liver?" Reuben asked.

We left an hour later, driving back to Manhattan. Tony was simmering, but he didn't say a word for about thirty miles. He exploded on the Garden State Parkway. "Damn! I *knew* I shouldn't have brought you to that Reuben. He's crazier than you! And all that *I Ching* junk really deranged you. What is going *on,* Alice? What's all this nonsense with cooking classes? How do you know Dan Wu will agree? What are you up to?"

He slammed one hand on the wheel. I didn't answer.

"I know you went through something pretty bad. I know you loved that guy, Alice. So you ought to have enough sense to stop plotting for a while. You're just going to get yourself and others in trouble. The more this goes on, the more I think your boyfriend was right. That the whole thing was about powdered rhino horn, and you just can't see the forest for the trees."

All I could say was, "Trust me, Tony."

"No!" Tony shouted. "You trust *me*! You tell me what's going on."

"Soon, Tony, soon," I told him soothingly.

I started to massage the tight muscles in his neck with my left hand as he was driving. For some reason the movement of my hand and the feel of his neck made me think of Sonny. The rage and the shame came back, but along with them were sorrow and longing.

I started to cry.

"Please don't cry, Swede. I could never handle your crying," Tony pleaded.

I fought to control myself.

"Okay!" he shouted. "Listen, stop crying. From now on I don't say a goddamn word. Not a word. I am your faithful slave. You tell me what to do and I'll do it. Okay? I'll be Lancelot to your Guinevere. Just send me out on adventures. Your bidding is my command. Even dragons, Swede. Even those dragons in the *I Ching* hexagram—I'll fight for you."

"Thank you, Tony," was all I could say after I had stopped crying. We entered Manhattan and returned the rented car.

"What does my lady desire?" Tony asked, as we walked away from the rental place.

"A library," I replied. We walked to the Mid-Manhattan Library on 40th Street and Fifth Avenue. I obtained quickly, from a directory, the names and addresses of three New Jersey newspapers that publish Sunday editions in the greater Swedesboro area.

"Now what?"

"I need a press release, Tony. Do you know how to write press releases?"

Tony groaned. But as my knight-in-waiting, he could do no other than comply. He took me to a print shop in a dismal building on West 39th Street. It was a firm he used to do business with when he owned the Mother Courage Copy Shops, before he decided to return to the theater. A calm woman with tortoiseshell glasses asked me how many copies of the press release I needed. Ten, I said. She found that very funny, but she quoted me a most reasonable price. Then we moved to the word processor. She explained how it was done. Everything was laid out on the word processor, including the letterhead, then it was printed out, then reproduced in one uninterrupted sequence. Astonishing.

For the letterhead of the release I chose

The Softly Falcon Inn—Bed & Breakfast

and on the upper right-hand corner of the page I typed the address in Cape May and the phone number. The computer provided me with the silhouette of a falcon for the upper left-hand corner of the release.

For the headline of the press release I chose

FINALLY—SWEET PEANUT SOUP WITH STRAWBERRIES IN CAPE MAY!

It was catchy. The body of the release merely stated that the world-famous chef Dan Wu would be conducting a one-day, eight-hour seminar in Cape May at The Softly Falcon Inn on the following Wednesday. Students would learn the newest wrinkles in new-wave Chinese vegetarian cuisine. Applicants must call the Inn on Tuesday, the day before the seminar. Registration would be limited to the first fifteen to call, at a fee of two hundred and fifty dollars. Utensils and foodstuffs to be provided by Mr. Wu.

The press release looked marvelous, and I immediately mailed copies to the three New Jersey newspapers.

"Now what?" Tony asked.

"Now we part," I said. "I'll meet you in front of your hotel at nine o'clock Friday morning."

"To do what?"

"To pick up Dan Wu's cat."

"But we're not going out to Cape May again until Tuesday. Why doesn't the cat stay with Wu until then?"

"Remember your pledge," I cautioned. He made a sign that he was zippering his mouth shut.

I kissed him on the head and went home. I didn't want to think about anything. I just wanted to take care of my cats and clean the apartment, thank Mrs. Oshrin and tell her that I would need her services again the following week for a day or two. The cat-sitter who needs a cat-sitter for her own cats is a pain in the neck.

I listened to my recorded calls. Sonny had kept calling me, but his pleas were fading in intensity. He would not call many more times, I knew.

But my agent had made six frantic calls while I was gone.

I returned her call. She was ecstatic. Brian Watts had contacted her. The part was mine. He would be in New York with the contract during the first week of July. Shooting would probably begin in late October. Fine. Thanks. Stay in touch. And the call was over. It meant money, probably more money than I had ever seen. It meant, maybe, a breakthrough—a whole spate of well-paying movie roles. I really didn't give a damn. I just wanted to sleep and talk to my cats and not think about Sonny and get ready for Dan Wu's cooking class.

On Friday morning, as planned, I met Tony in front of his hotel on East 51st Street. Then we took a cab to the Upper East Side.

When Tony saw that the taxi had deposited us in front of the ASPCA building, he was dumbfounded. "I thought we were picking up Dan Wu's cat," he said.

"Dan Wu doesn't own a cat," I admitted. "I want you to go inside and adopt a cat or a kitten. We're going to give him or her a very good home."

"Aren't you coming in with me?"

"No, Tony, I can't handle it. I haven't been in the ASPCA since I got Pancho. I don't want to go in again. I don't want to see all those strays."

"What do I need?" he asked.

"Nothing. Just identification. And some money to pay for the shots. And a good heart."

"But what kind of cat do you want?"

"Pick the one you think will most appreciate a good home."

"Thanks," he said sarcastically, and walked inside.

He came out ten minutes later without a cat.

"What's the problem?" I asked.

"I can't make a selection."

"Why not?"

"Well, if it's so easy, *you* go in and try."

"I told you I can't go in there."

"Okay, okay . . ." He walked back inside, muttering, angry.

Twenty minutes later he came back out, holding a large cardboard carrier.

His face was pale. He looked frightened. Whatever was inside the box was hissing and clawing and shaking the box like Jell-O.

We walked half a block together; Tony, myself, and the wildcat inside the box—until Tony could go no further.

"Put the box down and relax," I said.

He followed instructions and appeared greatly relieved. "I had the feeling Mugsy would be a bit much."

"Mugsy? Who is Mugsy?"

"The cat in the box," Tony said.

"What a stupid name for a cat," I replied.

"Not when you take a look at him," Tony explained.

Down on the ground, the cat in the box had begun to calm down. At least he was no longer trying to rip the cardboard apart.

I crouched next to the box to peep through some of the airholes.

A pair of the angriest chartreuse eyes I have ever seen glared back at me.

"Now, Mugsy," I cooed, "just take it easy. Remember that God loves you, Aunt Alice loves you, and even your Uncle Tony loves you."

My assurances of eternal love elicited another round of frenzied clawing from Mugsy.

I could see why Tony had named him Mugsy. He was a very powerful, low-to-the-ground, no-neck, discolored white alley cat, with one-third of one ear gone and enough scars to play tic-tac-toe on him. His coat was very short. His tail was very broad.

He was very angry; too angry to realize that we had saved his life. For a brief moment I was going to chastize Tony for not having selected a kitten, but I kept my mouth shut. After all, I had refused to make the selection. And who was I to say that Mugsy didn't deserve to live out the rest of his life in peace just because he was a bit old, more than a bit ugly, and a bit unsociable?

We took a cab back to the hotel and, once outside on the street in front of the hotel, Tony panicked. "How am I going to get the cat inside? No pets are allowed . . . none at all. Not even turtles."

"Calm down, Tony," I said. "I'll show you in a minute. But first here's a list of what you'll need for Mugsy." I slipped the paper into his pocket. "Now," I ordered, "put the carrier down and take off your jacket." He did so. "Now pick up the carrier." He did so. "Now fold the jacket over the carrier and just walk inside to the elevator. No one will know a thing."

As we walked through the entrance he cast me a glance that told me he would continue to follow all my instructions blindly, but no longer happily.

I went back to my apartment, hoping to spend the next few days soaking up silence and calmness before I sprung the trap.

Alas, it was not to be. Tony started calling every two hours or so from his hotel room. First Mugsy wouldn't eat. Then Mugsy was gorging himself. Then Mugsy was about to attack him. Then Mugsy seemed to be making sexual advances. And after each complaint came the question, "What do I *do*?"

Of course I gave him my best advice as each crisis arose. Of course he was just having a minor nervous breakdown—Tony, that is. Mugsy seemed to be doing just fine.

And then Tony became obsessed that the cleaning woman was about to discover Mugsy. What should he do? I advised him just not to admit the cleaning lady until we left for Cape May on Tuesday morning. That was unacceptable to him, so he began to enlist other guests on his floor in a plot to hide Mugsy during the cleaning lady's stint in his room.

Would Tuesday never come?

24

Tuesday did come, and we left New York in a rented car very early in the morning—the three of us.

By eight-thirty, Tony, Mugsy, and I were standing in the hallway of The Softly Falcon Inn before a beaming Reuben Tarnapol.

"Is that Dan Wu's cat?" he asked.

"Yes," I lied.

"Then where's Dan Wu?"

"He'll be here tomorrow, just in time for the class," I lied.

Reuben stared admiringly at the squat white cat.

"She's beautiful," he noted.

"It's a he," Tony corrected. "His name is Mugsy."

"I have a present for you," Reuben said gleefully, and it took me a few seconds to realize that "you" meant the cat. He vanished into the kitchen and came back quickly, opening the large package in his hand as he walked.

"Look!" he called out to Mugsy. Reuben then held up a long, extremely odorous piece of raw liver, which was exuding blood.

Mugsy reacted as any self-respecting cat would.

First he sat down, in that strange, calm posture

that cats strike just before they commence a hunt, as if they are gathering all their energy. His eyes were unflinchingly on his prey, and one of his ears and the tip of his tail had begun a slight twitch.

Then Mugsy moved forward, low to the ground, as if he were bellying through grass: powerful, fast, focused. He leaped and ripped the slab of meat from Reuben's hand, and ran through the dining room and into the kitchen.

Blood, of course, followed him. But no matter—Reuben was even more ecstatic than Mugsy.

"That was spectacular!" he crowed. "But now I have to get out to the birds. So let me show you how I rigged up the video cameras."

We walked through the dining room and into the kitchen, where Mugsy was ripping the liver to shreds. Reuben had done a masterful job. The bottom third of the heretofore open doorway between the kitchen and storeroom was now blocked by a slab of wood, and the top two-thirds had been covered by curtains. The video cameras were mounted behind them, their snouts pointing into the kitchen through slashes in the curtain.

"You see," he explained, "no one in the kitchen can tell what those things are. They might be exhaust pipes. They might be air-conditioning ducts. No one will press the case further." He grinned, then said, "Follow me." We walked back through the dining room, out the front door, around the side of the house, and stopped by the outside entrance to the storeroom.

"Tomorrow morning, when the class starts, just enter this way with this key, walk inside, activate the cameras, then go out the same way and lock the door behind you."

He opened the door and we walked in. The cameras were rigged on ladders. Ingenious. "Look here. You see this timer on this ladder rung? When you're ready to start shooting, you flip it all the way to the left." I nodded. It looked like a model train switch.

"I had to modify my original plan," he said apologetically. "Originally I thought all four cameras could run sequentially. But I wasn't thinking clearly. Even with jumbo cartridges, there might not be enough tape that way. So I rigged them to run two at a time. Once you flip the switch, two cameras turn on and run for twenty minutes. Then they shut off automatically and the other two kick in. Then the first two again. Get it? You won't get as wide a sweep with two running at one time as if four were running—but they'll do the trick, and they're sure. Once we get the tape, we can edit it any way we want."

He gave me the key and left. I studied the placement of the cameras for a while, then went back outside and into the Inn through the front door. Tony was on his way out. He was going, he said, to explore the village.

I was alone in the house with Mugsy. I smiled when I remembered that Reuben had called him "beautiful." I love all cats, and I truly loved Mugsy, but only an ex-actor who yearned to be an Eastern mystic and had ended up a bird-watcher could have characterized Mugsy as beautiful.

All three of the rural newspapers must have picked up my fake press release and run it prominently in their Sunday editions, because the phone started to ring at ten A.M. with very eager gourmands who wanted to join Dan Wu's cooking class the following day.

To each one who called, I relayed the same message: "Dan Wu regrets that he has had to cancel the class due to personal problems."

Judging by the groans on the other end of the phone, it appeared to be a major disappointment to all concerned. By the time Reuben and Tony returned from their travels, the calls had slowed down. To cover myself, I told all other callers that the class had already been filled. Reuben and Tony were much impressed.

That evening I took them both out to dinner. We went to a small bar and grill right by the ocean. It had terrible food but a wonderful jukebox. Tony just seemed to want to drink brandy and eat littleneck clams with a great deal of horseradish on each. Reuben consumed vast amounts of french-fried onion rings, downed by quaff after quaff of white wine. He was a very odd Eastern mystic indeed.

By the time we all got back to the Inn my two companions had been overcome by their drinking efforts, and they retired immediately. Everything was going well.

I went to my room around ten and sat on the bed, fully clothed, staring at the face of my traveling alarm clock.

The trap had been well set. I was confident. But for the first time, my nerves were beginning to jangle. I knew *they* would come that very night. But did I really know who *they* were? I had a very strong sense of why they would come. But did I really know what they would do . . . what they were capable of? Had I really only set a trap for myself?

At eleven, I walked quietly downstairs. I switched on a small light in the dining room and another in the kitchen. Any intruders would think them normal nightlights—and they would provide enough light for the video cameras to record.

Then I slipped through the front door and circled the house. I smiled when I noticed that all the windows on the ground floor of the house were half-open. It seems people just don't close their windows in Cape May in the spring. That was very good. There would be no need for a violent break-in.

I opened the storeroom door from the outside, located the switch that controlled the video cameras, and flicked it to the on position. Then I locked the door and walked back around the house, through the front door, and up the steps.

The back of my neck was beginning to tingle. I was also beginning to feel that tinge of nausea that always comes before a performance.

I put my ear against Reuben's door. He was snoring heavily. Nothing would wake him.

Then I opened the door to Tony's bedroom and walked inside quickly, shutting the door behind me. He was asleep, but he always sleeps lightly. I could see Mugsy curled up near the bed. Moonlight was filtering in between the bed and the cat.

"Tony!" I whispered urgently.

He got up immediately and switched on the small light near the bed. He was dazed. "What's the matter?"

"Nothing." I sat down beside him on the bed. "I just have to talk to you for a minute."

He sat up. "Sure. Talk."

"There will be no cooking class with Dan Wu

tomorrow, Tony. There will be no cooking class at all."

"Why not?"

"It's all a fake. The press releases, everything. It's a trap, Tony."

"For who?"

"You'll find out soon, Tony. Someone is going to break into this house tonight."

"Are you sure?"

"It will be sometime between midnight and just before dawn, I imagine."

"Are you going to call the police?"

"No, Tony. There will be no danger to us. They must be left alone, and not interrupted. The video cameras will record them without their knowing."

"I really hope you know what you're doing with all this, Alice."

"Tony, it is very important that they are not interrupted . . . that this play itself out. Do you understand? And it's going to be difficult for both of us, lying in our respective beds, knowing the trap is laid, waiting for those first sounds of entry. It would be better if we were both asleep."

"Well, I'll try to get back to sleep, but you'll have to give me a few minutes," he said, laughing.

Then he enthusiastically kissed me on the neck and whispered, "Such a beautiful woman, but so like my mother. She used to tell me that if I didn't go to sleep, Santa would never come."

I stood and smiled at him.

"There's one other thing, Tony. I'd like Mugsy to sleep downstairs."

"But you said someone will break in tonight. I don't want him hurt."

"Believe me, Tony. Nothing bad will happen to Mugsy."

I opened the door wide and Mugsy scampered out. He would, of course, go down to the kitchen, where all those good smells reside and where all those cool tiles waited for him.

I went back to my room and set my alarm for six o'clock. Then I lay down wondering how long it would take me to get to sleep.

The next thing I knew the tiny clock was buzzing into my ear like a crazed bumblebee. I shut the alarm off and peered out the small window, dazed.

Yes, it was almost morning. The sky was a half-gold, half-black soup.

I walked quickly into Tony's room and woke him. He dressed in an instant, except for his shoes, which remained unlaced.

Slowly, we walked down the stairs together. It was spooky. The only sounds in the house were our feet softly crunching on the steps.

At the base of the steps, Tony peered into the living room and the dining room.

"Nothing seems out of place," he whispered.

"The kitchen, Tony. We have to go into the kitchen."

'This is like Christmas morning," Tony whispered, almost giggling.

The giggle died in his throat the moment we switched on the full kitchen light.

"My God!" he cried out, grabbing my arm.

We both stared at the orgy of bright red and green spraypaint that crisscrossed the kitchen—on the walls, on the ceiling, on the floors, on the cabinets, and on the enormous range.

"Who got in here last night? What kind of madmen?"

"They aren't madmen, Tony. They were just trying out their penmanship."

"Penmanship?"

"Yes. You are looking at a number of variations on the Chinese character for soup."

Tony no longer seemed to be listening. He started moving wildly about the kitchen, back and forth. "Where's Mugsy? What happened to my cat?"

"He's gone, Tony."

"Gone? *Gone?*" He was furious. "You let him out of the room last night and you told me nothing would happen to him! You told me he would be safe!"

"Calm down, Tony. He was taken by our visitors. You mustn't worry. Believe me, our visitors love cats. Your friend Mugsy will have a new home more luxurious than in his wildest dreams. Plenty of feline companions. Plenty of field mice. Plenty of affection, if he wants it."

Tony threw up his hands in confusion. He shook his head from side to side. He sat down, then stood up again. He circled the kitchen, then stood still. "What is poor Reuben going to make of all this?" he finally asked.

For some reason that question made me laugh, and keep on laughing.

25

It was eleven o'clock in the morning. Hardly the witching hour, but for some reason I had chosen to dress all in black, like a grieving widow, including a small black hat with a half-veil. I was waiting for Detective Rothwax in front of Dan Wu's building on West 23rd Street.

Rothwax was already ten minutes late, but I had expected that. He really hadn't wanted to meet me at all. He seemed to blame me for some emotional problems his star Eurasian detective was going through. He had been very curt and rude on the phone. God knows what Sonny had told him about me . . . about us.

It was only when I told him that I could give him the killer of the waitress in Dan Wu's restaurant, but would be glad to hand over that information to my local precinct if that was what he preferred . . . only then did he agree to meet me.

He arrived twenty minutes late, gruff and entirely unapologetic.

"This had better be good, Cat Woman," he threatened.

I smiled sweetly and led him into the building, up to Dan Wu's suite of offices. I had made an appointment by phone, so I knew that Wu was waiting . . . although he didn't know for what.

The Great Chef was smiling and gracious behind his elegant desk. He was wearing a black silk shirt and tan trousers.

I introduced him to Detective Rothwax. Wu's eyes narrowed ever so slightly. He knew that Rothwax was Sonny Hoving's superior, and Sonny had been unceasing, albeit unsuccessful so far, in his efforts to nail Wu.

Rothwax and I sat down in chairs facing the desk. With a dramatic flourish, I placed on the bare table a copy of Wu's cookbook and a videotape. Wu said nothing; he kept smiling. Rothwax began to squirm, and it was to him I said in a clear, almost didactic tone, "I brought you here because Dan Wu knows who shot up his restaurant, and why. I think now he will tell you."

We both turned to Wu. The smile had left his face, and his shoulders had slumped. He did not speak.

I went on. "Mr. Wu has done nothing criminal, except protect the shooters. He believes that the shooting of the waitress was a tragic error. And he has strong emotional ties to the shooters. That is why he has not broken his silence." I paused and waited. Again no reply. "Am I correct, Mr. Wu?"

The Great Chef smiled again. "I don't know what you are talking about, Miss Nestleton."

"Do you have a VCR on the premises?" I asked.

"Of course," he replied.

"May we use it?"

Dan Wu stared at me, then at Rothwax, then at the objects I had placed on the table. He stood up, excused himself, and left the room. He returned quickly with an assistant, pushing a Sony color TV with accompanying VCR perched on a dolly. The assistant plugged the apparatus into the wall and left.

I closed the blinds of the two large windows without asking permission and inserted the tape.

I said to Rothwax, "A few days ago I planted fake press releases in three Southern New Jersey papers. The release stated that Dan Wu would be teaching an all-day course in Chinese vegetarian cooking at an inn in Cape May.

"The night before the class was supposed to be taught, four men broke into the premises at around three in the morning. Unbeknownst to them, they were being recorded by video cameras."

Then I ran the tape. It was wavy and dark. The various elements had been spliced together. But it told a coherent story.

Four men were standing inside the kitchen speaking softly in Chinese. Three of them were young. One was old—very old.

The three young men removed objects from their pockets. Not guns—spray cans. They proceeded to spray-paint all over the kitchen with a kind of manic energy.

"What the hell are they doing?" Rothwax asked, incredulous.

I froze the tape when the graffiti came clearly into view.

"Look at it closely, Detective Rothwax."

Rothwax left his seat and approached the screen, studying the strange marks.

"Do they look familiar?" I asked.

"Yes, they do," he admitted.

I glanced at Dan Wu. His arms were folded tightly across his chest, as if he had suddenly grown cold. He stared blankly at the videotape.

"Damn!" Rothwax suddenly exclaimed. He turned toward me, a look of triumph on his face. "That's the same mark that was left on the restaurant wall the night of the murder!"

"Right," I confirmed. "It is the Chinese character for soup. And the three young men wielding the spray cans in this video are the same young Chinese men who shot up the restaurant. I'm sure you'll find witnesses who can confirm that."

I started the tape again and stopped it when the old man was clearly visible. He was holding Mugsy tenderly in his arms.

"This man is Ch'in Shih," I said. Then I went to the table and picked up *Five Flavors*. I waved it at Rothwax and said, "If you had taken the time, Detective Rothwax, to read Dan Wu's book, you would know the name."

I started to run the tape again, but suddenly Dan Wu shouted, "Turn it off! Turn it off!" I did as he ordered.

He was standing behind his desk now, wild-eyed.

"Do you know the old man on the tape?" Rothwax asked him.

"Yes. He is my Master. But he is old and senile. He did not know what he was doing. They did not mean to kill that girl. I swear it."

Dan Wu sat down slowly. His face was bathed in sweat.

"What do you mean by your 'master'?" Rothwax asked.

"Ch'in Shih was one of the great chefs of Hong Kong, many years ago. He took me in as a child and taught me everything he knew. He cared for me as if he was my own father. But he grew tired of the kitchen. He was a man of the spirit . . . of the Tao. So together we journeyed to America and he purchased a small farm so he might live simply, close to the earth, as he wished to live."

Wu wiped the sweat off his face with the hem of his silk shirt. Then he continued.

"I grew bored with farm life. I was ambitious. So I went to the big city and became a famous chef. We remained close. We spoke all the time. He helped other young Chinese men; there were always orphaned children or illegal immigrants in his care.

"And then I decided to open a restaurant. He gave me his blessing. He even brought me one of his cats, a beautiful cat, because that is a tradition, to give a cat to a new restaurant venture to increase the harmony. For what is a restaurant without a kitchen cat? Who will guard the food from the mice?

"It was only after the restaurant had opened that he realized it would be a *vegetarian* restaurant. He was deeply offended. He was a great chef, and he believed that it was evil to concentrate on one kind of food. He believed that one must serve, at every meal, flesh and grain and vegetables. He believed that to concentrate on one kind of food was blasphemous to the Tao . . . to the Middle Way. He believed that there can be no harmony between man and the earth where only vegetarian food is served. At first I didn't take him seriously, and I thought he would get over his opposition. I explained to him that it was only a fad, that it was only a way for me to make enough money to open up more traditional restaurants. And besides, I told him, that was what the Americans wanted now . . . that Americans consider vegetables the most healthy of foods.

"But age had hurt his mind. He became bitter and vindictive. I stopped seeing him because he railed against my menu. He drew the Chinese character for soup on my menu and ripped it to pieces. For soup is the most harmonious of foods, and I had sinned against harmony. And then he threatened me. But I thought it was the threat of an impotent old man."

Wu buried his face in his hands for a moment. Then he looked up.

"Believe me! They didn't mean to shoot that girl. It was just a way to frighten me. To show me the spiritual dangers if I persisted. That's why his young charges took the kitchen cat away with them—the cat he himself had given me. The cat could no longer, in his view, reside in such an unharmonious place. He is an old man gone mad. But he did not mean harm. When I was a child, he would chastise me if I bruised even a fly."

Wu had finished speaking. He was exhausted, drained. Rothwax kept shaking his head, incredulous. I sympathized with him. It was hard to live with the idea of a girl dying because of an "unharmonious" menu. But there it was—the sad and amazing truth.

Rothwax sighed, picked up the phone, and dialed. The moment he began to speak I tensed. He was talking to Sonny Hoving. But all he said was, "I'm at Dan Wu's. You'd better get over here fast. And bring a recorder. Mr. Wu is going to make a statement."

"The videotape is yours, Detective Rothwax," I said, standing up and preparing to leave.

"Where are you going? What's your rush?"

"The Cat Woman has other fish to fry," I said, mockingly.

As I left, I saw Wu look at me once. There was anger in his eyes. As if I had offended against the Tao.

I was already on the street when I remembered that I had left *Five Flavors* on Dan Wu's desk. I didn't want to go back for it. Anyway, I knew I would be taking a vacation from Chinese food for a while, and I was in a hurry to meet Basillio and tell him what I had forgotten to tell him in Cape May: that I was about to become a movie star.

Of course, I knew exactly what he would say in reply: "Well Swede, it's about time you sold out. We could both use a new pair of shoes."

As I walked to meet Tony at our prearranged rendezvous—a bakery/coffee shop on 21st Street east of Broadway—I realized that I had another stop to make first. A stop I was duty-bound to make. I had to go see the mother of Nancy Han and tell her that before the day was finished, that lunatic Taoist goon squad comprised of Ch'in Shih and his harmonious machine-gunners would be behind bars, charged with the murder of her daughter.

That was the least I could do. Tony would wait. He would eat croissants and apricot jam. He would be patient.

I hailed a cab.

26

Mrs. Han kept the inside chain on the door as she peered through the opening at me. It seemed to take her the longest time to remember just who I was—the woman who had delivered her daughter's belongings and made such a fuss over her cat.

Then she nodded, and as she was unfastening the chain said to me in the most polite tone possible, "It would be best to call first. I am often not home in the afternoon, and your trip would be in vain."

I apologized. She accepted my apology graciously and ushered me inside, to the same two straight-backed chairs that faced each other.

Millie was lying peacefully in one corner of the room, observing me. My eyes filled with tears. It was the first time I had had the leisure to truly observe her, and her resemblance to my grandmother's Henrietta. It was an astonishing likeness, if my childhood memories were accurate.

I sat down, and, just as she had before, she asked me if I would like some tea. I declined.

Mrs. Han folded her hands together and waited. She did not sit down. I could tell by her puffy face that the grief had not left her. Perhaps it never would.

"Mrs. Han, the men who murdered your daughter are going to be brought to justice. The police know who they are now. Dan Wu, the owner of the restaurant your daughter worked in, has identified them.

She didn't reply.

"I know nothing can ease the pain of your daughter's death. It was a terrible thing. It could have been anyone. Bullets were flying all around. They didn't mean to kill her. But they are murderers, and they deserve what they are going to get."

Then she sat down on the chair and the tears began to roll down her face. I told her everything. I told her what had transpired in Dan Wu's office: my showing of the video; Rothwax's comments; Wu's final confession that he knew who had shot up the restaurant and why; and Wu's decision not to protect his guru anymore.

I told her how that crazy old man Ch'in Shin had resorted to violence just because an ancient cooking principle had been violated by an ambitious, well-meaning student.

I told Nancy Han's mother everything, and the more I spoke the more I felt I was doing some good . . . bringing this woman some solace. At least she would now comprehend the events that had led up to this tragedy. It wouldn't lessen the hurt, but. . .

Suddenly, Millie streaked across the room and leaped lightly into Mrs. Han's lap. I smiled. Mrs. Han stroked Millie with one hand.

I should leave, I thought. I have done what I had to do. I started to get up, but Mrs. Han made a slight motion with one hand to indicate that I should remain seated.

I waited.

She said in a soft voice, "What a fool you are."

I was so startled by her words that all I could say was, "Pardon me?"

"Do you really believe all that nonsense you told me?"

"I told you the truth, Mrs. Han. You can verify it by contacting a Detective Rothwax of the NYPD. He's at Dan Wu's office right now.

"Fool," she repeated. Then she said it again in a louder voice.

Then she screamed *"Fool!"* with such power and hatred that Millie flew out of her lap to the far end of the room and I positively cringed in my chair.

She got up, walked to a lovely chest, opened it, and returned holding a small object in her hand.

It was a gun.

An ugly little silver-plated derringer.

I felt absolutely powerless. Frightened. Bewildered.

Mrs. Han put the gun close to my head. Her face had become composed, almost serene.

"Fools like you should die," she said.

I wanted to pray. I tried to remember that psalm, but all I could think of was, "He leadeth me beside the still waters."

Then Mrs. Han said, "Go!" She stepped aside. I ran from the apartment and down the steps, and didn't stop running until I was a hundred feet from the entrance.

There was a telephone booth across the street. I crossed over and began to fumble for change, though I hadn't the slightest idea whom to call, or why.

Gradually my fear abated. But I couldn't fathom

what had happened, nor did I know what to do next.

Then Mrs. Han emerged from the building.

I stepped back, so that the phone booth would hide me from her sight.

But she wasn't looking for me.

She stood for a moment, talking to herself, so obviously distraught that she appeared to be on furlough from a mental institution.

Then she started to walk uptown. She had one hand in her coat pocket, and she carried no purse.

I knew that ugly little derringer was in her pocket. And I had the horrible intuition that she was on her way to kill Dan Wu.

I don't know why I thought that, but I felt it strongly . . . I sensed it. It had something to do with her calling me a fool.

She began to walk west. I followed her. She reached Broadway and turned north. I kept on. She seemed to be engaged in an inner dialogue with herself, alternately stopping in the street and then starting up again. From time to time she stared at herself in store windows, but she never took her hand out of her pocket.

For a moment I doubted my original perception—that she was going to kill Dan Wu. After all, it's a very long walk from the tip of Manhattan Island up to 23rd Street—a very long walk indeed.

But Mrs. Han kept walking. And I saw that tears were rolling down her face again. She started to walk faster.

I couldn't afford to wait any longer. I stopped at a pay phone and dialed Dan Wu's office. Sonny Hoving answered the phone. In the background I could hear Rothwax yelling at someone.

"Sonny, it's Alice. Nancy Han's mother has gone crazy. She threatened me with a gun. She's walking uptown now, and I get the feeling she has it in her mind to kill Dan Wu."

"Calm down, Alice," he said. I didn't even realize I was excited. "Listen to me, Alice. Just keep your distance from her. There are cops all over the street and in the building. Don't worry. We'll pick her up when she gets here. You just stay a safe distance away, okay?"

I hung up the phone. We were in the busy City Hall area, and I found it difficult to keep Mrs. Han in sight. But as we moved north, the crowds thinned for a while.

Then we reached Canal Street. Only about thirty more blocks, I thought grimly. Mrs. Han seemed to be sleepwalking now, walking slowly but resolutely.

Why, I kept thinking, did she call me a fool?

Suddenly, Mrs. Han was gone. I stopped in my tracks, staring wildly about me like a lost child. She had simply slipped out of my sight.

Had she crossed the street? I searched the storefronts on the other side. No, she had just vanished.

Then I saw her again, walking with a new spring in her step. She had turned off Canal and was walking east on a side street.

I looked at the street sign. It was Broome Street.

I froze. My God! I had gotten it all wrong. She wasn't going to Dan Wu. She was going to Anna Li—the hostess who lived on Broome and the Bowery.

There was a pay phone on the far side of Canal. I ran across the street and dialed Dan Wu's office again. Sonny answered. I said: "Sonny! She's not going up there. She's going to the hostess—Anna Li."

"Where are you, Alice?" He asked.

"Canal and Broome."

"Now listen to me carefully, Alice. Are you listening?"

"Yes. Yes!"

"Stay exactly where you are. I'll drive right down now. I'll be there in five minutes. Do you hear me, Alice? Stay where you are!"

I hung up and waited. The weather was balmy, but I had become chilled.

He arrived in less than five minutes, screeching around the corner in an unmarked brown police car with one of those portable strobe lights blinking on the hood. He flung the far-side door open.

I yelled to him, "It's a one-way street, Sonny—you're going the wrong way!"

"Shut up and get in!" He yelled back. I slid into the seat next to him. He reached across me and slammed the door shut. For just a moment he kept his arm pressed against me, then he brought his hand back to the wheel.

"Show me the place," he said and we took off, oblivious to the fact that we were going the wrong way on Broome and scaring oncoming drivers half to death.

We were there in seconds. Sonny leaped out of the car and I followed.

The moment we entered the small lobby we heard the shot.

Sonny reached down to his ankle holster and pulled out his gun. Then he kicked the inside door open with one savage blow.

"Stay here, Alice!" he yelled, and ran up the stairs. I followed him.

Mrs. Han was standing outside Anna Li's apartment. The outside door was open, but that strange inner glass door was still closed.

The glass, however, had been shattered. Through its spiderwebbed patterns, I could just make out the crumpled form of Anni Li on the floor.

Mrs. Han had shot the hostess through the glass door.

"Let the gun fall to the floor!" Sonny screamed at the woman. She didn't do anything. Then he shouted at her in Chinese. Still she didn't respond. Sonny then slapped the gun from her hand and threw her hard against the wall.

"Watch her!" he ordered me.

Sonny used the butt of his gun to smash through a section of the shattered glass, then reached through to open the door from the inside. Once inside, he knelt beside the fallen woman, his hand searching for an arterial pulse.

"She's dead," he announced. He went to the phone and punched 911. Then he went back to the body and tried mouth-to-mouth resuscitation. I brought Mrs. Han inside the apartment, leaving the weapon outside on the floor in the hallway. I was breathing heavily. I couldn't bear to look at the body.

"No use," Sonny said, sitting back and staring at Anna Li. "No use at all. She was dead when she hit the floor."

He looked curiously at Mrs. Han.

"Why did you do this?" he asked.

"She murdered my daughter," Mrs. Han said calmly.

"No, Mrs. Han," Sonny replied wearily. "A young man in the employ of Ch'in Shih shot your daughter."

Then she started to sob, a sudden squall of tears washing over her. She fought for control, drying her cheeks with her sleeves.

"What fools you all are," she said. "What fools."

"*I'm* a fool?" Sunny blurted out, cruelly. "You're facing Murder One, and *I'm* a fool!" He shook his head sadly and started to walk toward me.

"She deserved to die," Mrs. Han whispered in a flat voice. "She was a criminal. She corrupted all the young people who worked there."

Sonny stopped and gave me a startled glance. Then he turned back to Mrs. Han. He said, "I'm going to place you under arrest now. And I'm going to read you your rights." But he did no such thing. He waited.

Mrs. Han said, "Only you fools didn't know. She told my Nancy that all she had to do was deliver those little paper bags to Boston and Scranton and Philadelphia. And Nancy did it. And the other girls did it. And she gave Nancy seven hundred and fifty dollars for every trip. I told Nancy to stop, but she wanted the money. And she said there was no danger, that everyone did it. Even Dan Wu's assistant . . . that man Jack Pallister. Everyone knew what was going on but Dan Wu. He is another fool, that man. A saint maybe, but a fool."

Sonny threw me another glance, this one perplexed, almost accusatory.

My whole case seemed to be collapsing with each word the woman spoke.

In desperation I said, "Anna Li was a brave woman. I was there that night in the restaurant.

She was the only one who tried to stop the gunmen; she was the only one in the entire restaurant who confronted them."

"Fool!" she spat out yet again. "You do not speak Chinese. She lied to the gunmen because she was so frightened. She lied to the gunmen to save herself. She told them that my daughter Nancy Han was the one who controlled the rhino horn smuggling. She knew why they were in the restaurant: to warn them that the operation must stop because it was the province of the Hong Kong people. So Anna Li gave them my daughter . . . who was only a messenger. And they killed her, on purpose. They murdered her. Only fools like you and Dan Wu did not know. Only fools like you and the police."

Then we heard the sound of footsteps on the stairs—the wheels of justice beginning to turn. The crime-scene photographers came and took pictures. The precinct cops came and took Mrs. Han. The EMS people came and took all that was left of Anna Li.

Then the apartment emptied out except for Detective Rothwax, Detective Hoving, and myself.

Sonny and I remained silent. Rothwax was pacing. When he stopped, he looked at me sharply and said, "We have a mess here, don't we, Cat Woman? We have to sort this mess out, don't we, Cat Woman?" He was angry—very angry.

"No," I replied softly, "there is no mess. We just have to make a few adjustments."

"Is that so, Cat Woman?" he said, the sarcasm dripping. "Well, why don't you go ahead and adjust."

I did so. "Dan Wu knew that Ch'in Shih had shot up his restaurant, but he didn't really know why. Oh, he knew that Jack Pallister was dealing in rhino horn, but he had no idea there was a widespread smuggling scheme operating out of his restaurant, masterminded by his hostess. Nor could he imagine his revered teacher Ch'in Shih working for Hong Kong smugglers and criminals. So when Dan Wu, after seeing my videotapes, decided it was time to blow the whistle on the old man, he settled on the only reason that made sense to him. A crazed old man hated him because he had sinned against the harmony of Chinese cookery . . . because he had bowed to American nouvelle cuisine and opened a totally vegetarian Chinese restaurant, something which, according to Ch'in Shih, degrades the Tao. In fact, Detective Rothwax, I believed Dan Wu's version as well."

"Damn it! I know the mistake Dan Wu made. And *you* made. But Dan Wu had an excuse. His old teacher shoots up a restaurant and paints the Chinese character of soup all over the wall. Who wouldn't believe the shooting had something to do with soup . . . with food . . . with harmony . . . with some damn crazy thing like that? The question I want you to answer for me, Cat Woman, is: Why did that old smuggler paint the goddamn soup character on the wall if he was interested in scaring Dan Wu into stopping a rival smuggling operation? And *why* did he take that stupid cat?"

"Calm down, Detective Rothwax, you're shouting," I reprimanded him, then looked to Sonny for support. None was forthcoming.

I explained. "The old man believed that Dan Wu was running the horn-smuggling operation. What could he paint on the wall—a charging rhino? A sexual organ? No; the soup character, he thought, would be enough to show Dan Wu that the harmony between master and teacher had been destroyed. The old man believed that symbol would be threatening enough. But since Dan Wu himself *wasn't* smuggling, and had no idea that his revered old teacher was a Hong Kong thug in mufti, he simply took the symbol at face value. Along with all the other angry remonstrances the old man had made to him. Dan Wu knew that Ch'in Shih despised his restaurant, but he had no idea why, so he had to assume, finally, it was because of the vegetarian angle. I assumed the same thing."

"And Mrs. Han?" Rothwax asked. "Why in hell, if she knew that Anna Li pointed her daughter out to the shooter, didn't she tell us, or you, or anyone?"

I looked quickly at Sonny and then back to Rothwax. "A certain Eursaian detective once told me that people like Mrs. Han only tell white investigators what they want to hear. Besides, the woman had just lost the most precious thing on earth to her—her daughter. Was she going to tell strangers that her daughter had been a criminal? Hardly. And I think Mrs. Han had no idea at all that the kind old Chinese man who delivered a cat to her as a condolence gift was a rhino-horn smuggler. Or had sent the shooters. Mrs. Han didn't care who pulled the trigger. She knew it was Anna Li who had guided the bullet. So when I told her that the old man was being charged with her daughter's murder, all she could think of was that the real—in her mind—murderer was about to get off scot-free. She cracked. She took her own vengeance."

"And the cat?" Rothwax asked.

"Just like Dan Wu said. The old man had his gunmen remove the cat because the harmony of the restaurant had been destroyed—it had become the center of a rival smuggling operation. Ch'in Shih had presented the cat to Dan Wu in good faith, and now he was removing it. The Lord giveth and the Lord taketh away. Even among Taoists."

Rothwax turned to Sonny. "Does what she just said make any sense?"

Sonny responded, "I can't give you an objective answer. You see, the Cat Woman and I were once very close."

There was an uncomfortable silence. I had never wanted to console Sonny more than at that moment. But I was also sure that whatever had been between us was now over . . . finished.

I started to leave.

"Where are you going?" Rothwax asked.

"Well, Detective Rothwax, you have a lot of work to do, you and all the people at RETRO. You have to charge Mrs. Han with the murder of Anna Li. You have to charge the old man and his thugs with the murder of Nancy Han. And you have to excavate the remains of two rival smuggling and distribution operations. But as for me, I have only one simple task to perform. I have to go back downtown to Mrs. Han's apartment, pick up a lovely red tabby cat, and take her back to her home."

Rothwax waved me out disgustedly. Sonny did not even look at me.

27

Once again Tony and I were in a rented car, driving south on the New Jersey Turnpike. I was calm, almost happy. Millie was nestled in my lap, just as Henrietta used to nestle in my grandmother's. Millie knew she was going home.

But Tony . . . ah, he was grumpy.

He kept saying things like, "You know, Swede, you really are beginning to irritate me. How do you *know* we'll find Mugsy alive and well? How can you be so damn sure?"

"Trust your Aunt Alice," I kept saying, trying to calm him.

"Right. A crazed, violent old smuggler, who is also some kind of Taoist holy man, kidnaps poor Mugsy from a Cape May kitchen, and you tell me not to worry."

"You must relax, Tony. Ch'in Shih kidnapped Mugsy for the same reason he removed Millie from the restaurant. He believed Dan Wu had desecrated the master/disciple relationship. Forget that he believed Dan Wu was smuggling. Forget the motive, Tony. The old man loves cats. Millie was one of his cats. He gave her to Dan Wu as a treasured gift. He that giveth can taketh. Besides, criminals sometimes are great animal lovers. And they're often sentimental. After all, when Ch'in

Shih found out that the wrong person had been killed . . . that Nancy Han was only a low-level messenger . . . he was so grieved that he gave her mother his precious Millie for company.

"I remember reading once about a famous Taoist priest who was also a swordsman. Taoist priests are not Buddhists. They will fight. That is part of the Middle Way. If you have to fight, you fight. Anyway, this priest literally laid down his life to save his pet cricket."

"A *cricket*?" Tony shouted. "We're talking about a big old alley cat!"

I shut up. It was futile to try to reason with Tony when he was in such a state. I scratched Millie behind one ear. She purred. "Ignore him," I whispered to her.

When Tony left the turnpike, we got lost as usual. But when we finally pulled up to The Good Taste Farm, it seemed not to have changed one iota. A kindly Chinese man greeted me with a bow, and Tony with a handshake through the window. It was apparent that he was only caretaking, since Ch'in Shih and his cohorts were all in jail.

The moment I opened the door, Millie flew out of the car and bounded away through the grass, no doubt looking for the nieces and nephews that we had seen in their kittenish tumbling the last time we had visited.

"We just stopped by for a minute," Tony explained. "We're looking for Mugsy." Our host obviously hadn't the slightest idea what Tony was talking about.

"Look there! Look there!" Tony suddenly shouted, pointing at the sweet little white-frame farm house.

I looked.

Sitting placidly on the low porch was none other than Sir Mugsy himself, watching the proceedings.

Tony was absolutely beside himself with glee. He reached into his pocket and pulled out a small, tightly wound bundle.

He started to walk quickly toward the house, unwrapping the bundle as he went, calling to me to follow him. He stopped three feet away from Mugsy, grinning, and finished the unwrapping. In his hand was a piece of raw, bloody liver.

"Look what I brought for you, Mugsy!" he said enthusiastically, waving the meat.

Mugsy rose very slowly, stretched, yawned, then ambled toward the intruder.

He sniffed the liver once, raised his tail, then turned and walked slowly and disdainfully away, vanishing behind the house.

Tony was utterly crestfallen. I took his hand. "Mugsy has learned to eat harmoniously," I explained. "After all, he's a Taoist now."

Hand in hand, we walked slowly back to the car.

The country road was empty. It was six in the morning. A dull gray spring morning. The red jeep bounced merrily along. On the stereo deck was Patsy Cline singing "I Fall to Pieces." Deirdre Quinn Nightingale had both hands on the wheel, one hand tapping time to the music with one finger. Charlie Gravis sat next to her, his head slumped, his eyes closed.

Didi, as she was called, felt very good. Howard Danto had called the night before and asked her to come over. He had some problems with his goat herd. And Howard Danto was one of the "new money" breeders and farmers in the town of Hillsbrook, Dutchess County, New York. It was the first time since Didi had returned home to open a veterinary practice a year ago that one of these new money people had called for her services.

Most of her clients in the past year had been old-line, struggling dairy farmers who had known her mother and Didi as a child. She loved them all dearly, but they didn't pay their bills and were extremely cynical toward the entire science of veterinary medicine. Oh, they used state-of-the-art milking machinery and computer-generated feed mixes . . . and when they were ill (the humans), they availed themselves of the latest in diagnostic and surgical techniques.

But when it came to one of their cows, they had the fatalism of fourteenth-century bedouins.

Danto would be different—she just knew it. She had heard he was interested in making the best soft goat cheese in the world and that he would pay anything to accomplish this. Sure, dairy cow operations were what a rural vet was all about in New York State; and this was what Didi wanted to do and she was happy—but she needed to expand her practice, both financially and intellectually. Howard Danto would be a beginning. After Danto might come one of those new thoroughbred horse breeding operations which had recently arrived in the county. Didi smiled, almost longingly. She could visualize herself entering one of those beautiful, enormous, wood-paneled stables—twenty yearlings, all in a row, waiting for her . . . multimillion-dollar babies sired by Seattle Slew and Alydar and Danzig and Mr. Prospector. Yes, she felt good.

"Could you lower it a bit, Miss Quinn?" Charlie Gravis asked.

"I thought you were asleep, Charlie," Didi said breezily, making no effort to lower the volume of Patsy Cline.

"Hard to sleep with this racket, Miss Quinn," Charlie replied, now staring out of the window and shaking his head slowly as if it were impossible to truly explain things to such a difficult young woman. He always called her by her mother's maiden name.

Didi kept driving. Should she lower the volume or not? If one gave Charlie an inch, he took a yard. A yard, he took half the circumference of the earth. Old Charlie Gravis was a problem. She had inherited the seventy-one-year-old man from her mother, along with three other rural people who had lived and worked on her mother's estate (if one could call it that) for years. When her mother died and Didi returned home, she simply didn't know what to do with them. They weren't paid salaries, just room and board. And they kept the place in order, after a fashion. So Didi had kept them on, as a sign of respect to her mother's memory. And she had made Charlie Gravis her veterinary assistant.

In retrospect, it had been a mistake. The retainers did exactly as they pleased. They kept a small herd of hogs for meat even though Didi didn't want hogs slaughtered on the premises. They took potshots at woodchuck and deer even though Didi told them not to. Yes, they were a problem—Charlie Gravis, Mrs. Tunney, Abigail, and Trent Tucker.

As for Charlie as a veterinary assistant: well, he was still strong and dependable in many ways, but he considered himself the dean of natural healers in the county. He had a herbal remedy for every animal disorder, from distemper to bee stings to foot rot, and he would regale her clients at the drop of a hat.

I must be logical, Didi thought. I must not let Charlie Gravis irritate me. I must think it out. Is the music too loud? If too loud, then turn it down. Didi contemplated the problem as the jeep sped along. She was sorry now she didn't have time for her breathing exercises before she left the house. Yoga in the early morning in the great outdoors always helped her meet the Charlie Gravis problem with ease. But there had been no chance. She had to be at Howard Danto's place on time, not only because she wanted to make a good impression on him, professionally, but because at eight o'clock in the morning she had to be at the Hillsbrook Diner to chair the local Committee On Rabies Control. She had to keep to schedule.

Didi looked over once at Charlie Gravis, sighed, and then leaned forward to turn the music down.

It was at this precise moment that the jeep hit one of those mud holes which have made upper Dutchess County, New York, the broken axle capital of the civilized world. The sturdy country road seemed to just give way and the jeep plunged crazily into a pit of moldering mud . . . bouncing the occupants around like coconuts. Five seconds later they were through it, unhurt, and on firm ground again.

The problem was, since it was a nice morning, Didi had kept the side flaps of the jeep open, and now both of them and the inside as well as the outside of the vehicle were covered with clumps of reddish mud. It had splattered all over them.

Didi pulled the jeep over to the side of the road to recover. She stared, or rather glared at Charlie Gravis, as if the whole thing were his fault. Then she burst out laughing.

Was she as covered with mud as Charlie? He looked like the Swamp Thing.

Five minutes later, cleaned up to the best of their ability, Didi and Charlie drove through the front gate of the Howard Danto farm.

The proprietor was waiting for them where the driveway ended. He was a huge man, in his late thirties, with an uncanny resemblance to the singer Burl Ives. He cradled a thermos in his meaty hand and the moment they stepped out of the jeep and introduced themselves to him, he poured them some coffee into paper cups. Didi was enchanted. Danto confirmed the old adage that while dairy farmers always dressed like dairy farmers, so-called gentleman farmers always dressed like *crazy* dairy farmers. It wasn't cold, but he had two mufflers around his neck and the most ragged pair of coveralls Didi had ever seen, over a bright red sweat shirt on which was printed PROPERTY OF SAN QUENTIN PRISON.

"Something very strange is happening to my goats," he said with genuine concern, an almost motherly pain in his voice.

"Well, let's take a look at them," Didi replied in her best professional manner, crumpling her paper cup and flinging it into the back of the jeep.

Off they trudged, Danto and Didi side by side. Charlie Gravis took up the rear, Charlie playing the role of scribe, carrying Didi's veterinary bag and the large notebook that she used to record her thoughts on examination and treatment.

As they walked, Howard Danto began to tell his story: how he had moved to the country after being a stockbroker in New York. And he began to outline his dream: How he was going to produce and market the finest soft goat cheese in the world from the finest goat's milk. He extolled the high, uniformly distributed butterfat content in his herd's milk. How he fed them no hay or prepared food, only forage all year long—brush, small trees, weeds, broadleaf plants—plus oats and corn and just a dollop of high-protein calf supplement for extra minerals and vitamins. How he had constructed various forage plots that could be closed off easily by strong, portable fences when a given area was overgrazed.

Didi smiled as she heard Charlie Gravis groan behind her. Old dairy farmers like him had nothing but bewildered contempt for wealthy, gentleman farmer visionaries like Danto. Didi appreciated Charlie's skepticism but she loved people like Danto, as much as she loved the old dairy farmers who struggled so hard and so long in no-win situations.

They passed the goat sheds and the milking stands and Danto pointed out the low green-and-white building in the distance which he called, with obvious pride, his "cheese factory."

Then they reached the herd. Didi immediately identified them as French Alpines—erect ears, long heads, straight or slightly dished noses. And the wide variety of colors were there—brown-and-white, black-and-white, solids. It wasn't a small herd either: more than twenty animals, mostly does with a scattering of kids and a buck or two.

Didi felt a surge of well-being as she contemplated the goats foraging around her. The wisdom of her decision to return home, assume the responsibility of her mother's property rather than sell it, and become an old-fashioned rural vet (if Dutchess County could still be characterized as rural) was apparent to her. After graduating from veterinary school at the University of Pennsylvania, she had done a year's postgraduate work in India, of all places—half because she loved elephants dearly and half because she had to recover far away from the scene of a very unhappy love affair. When she returned to the U.S., she had a series of short-lived staff positions at large suburban dog-and-cat hospitals and posh equine centers that featured swimming pool therapy and sophisticated surgical and laser techniques for mending broken-down racehorses. She was dreadfully unhappy at all of them.

"My goats are butting each other," Danto whispered, as if it were terribly illicit erotic behavior. "Suddenly, for no reason, they butt each other, or me, or the side of a building, or a fence post."

"Well, Mr. Danto," Didi explained, "goats have a pecking order, like chickens. They will butt in the sheds, for example, to get their feed first."

"No," Danto replied, his voice rising, "not in the sheds. In the fields. There's plenty of food around for everyone. No, it's not that. Look, come over to Laura."

They walked over to Laura, a refined-looking doe, who was calmly and methodically stripping a low lying shrub.

Laura seemed to ignore them. Didi studied her. She looked very much the healthy French Alpine, a wide-backed milking doe with firm, good-colored udders, not too low slung.

"Just wait, just wait," Howard Danto said, speaking softly. "Any little bit of extra stress will get her going."

Laura had, at first, appeared unconcerned with the presence of strangers, but now she stopped feeding and stared curiously. Then she took a few steps. Then she stopped.

"Wait," Danto kept whispering, "and watch for it."

As if on cue, Laura shot forward and slammed her lovely head against Charlie Gravis's thigh. Charlie cursed and, with an instinctual old dairyman's response, smacked his hand hard against the doe's rump, knocking her sideways. Danto uttered a moan of psychic pain at lovely Laura's getting hit. Didi glared at Charlie reproachfully.

Danto recovered. "There, do you see? They all do it now. All of them, even the kids. And they all have welts on their sides to prove it."

Didi realized that it was, indeed, very strange goat behavior—not a butt head-on but more of a side head slam.

Her experience with goats was not extensive, but she knew the drill. She knew exactly what questions the examination had to answer. Vet school had indelibly imprinted them onto her brain.

Approaching Laura, with Charlie and Danto surrounding the doe to keep her steady, Didi commenced the hands-on examination, while at the same time eliciting information from Howard Danto.

Is Laura alert and inquisitive? Is Laura's appetite constant? Is she chewing her cud? Are her eyes bright, without discharge? Is her nose dry and cool? Is her coat clean and glossy? Any abscesses under the jaw? On the legs? Are her droppings firm and pelleted? Is her urine light brown—without traces of blood? Is her breathing regular? Is her gait steady? Is she favoring any one of her feet? Any changes in quantity or quality of milk yield? Any stringiness in her milk? Any undue sensitivity in her udders?

Didi stepped back. According to the textbook, this goat was healthy. She caught a glimpse of her watch. It was seven-fifteen. She had to be at that meeting. But she also had to do a good job for Howard Danto. She stared at the goat. Laura seemed unconcerned once again, going back to her bush. But she was making some sounds: bleating quietly, almost in a whisper.

"What do you think?" Danto asked, ever anxious.

"I don't know yet. She appears to be healthy," Didi replied. Danto shook his head sadly.

Didi remembered what her favorite professor, Hiram Bechtold, used to say over and over again: "In most animal work, symptoms are clinically meaningless—unless you don't know what the hell to do."

Didi grimaced. Her mind went back to the symptom: head slamming. It signified nothing to her.

But head *pressing* did. Had Laura really wanted to head press rather than head slam? If so, it could be C.C.N. That was always a possibility.

"Do they ever keep their heads pressed for a while against a hard object or another goat?" she asked.

"No," Danto replied.

"Have you noticed any sign of failing eyesight?"

"No."

"Are you sure?"

"Well, the kids stumble a bit. But . . ."

"You see, Mr. Danto, it could be C.C.N."

"What's that?" Danto asked eagerly.

"Cerebral cortico necrosis," Didi answered.

"Can it be cured?"

"Oh, easily. It's just a fancy term for thiamine deficiency. It's caused by a fungus that destroys the ability of the enzymes to produce thiamine. But there's a problem here. You see, the fungus is ingested with their feed. And nowadays, the fungus, for the most part, is found in hay. Yet you said you don't give your goats any hay whatsoever."

"No, I definitely don't feed them hay—any kind of hay," Danto said, obviously disappointed that it wasn't such an easily discoverable disorder.

Didi realized what she should do next—just take a whole lot of blood and stool samples from the goats and send them off to a lab. But she wanted to impress Danto now. She didn't want to do that tired vet thing. She wanted to show Danto that while she might be young and relatively inexperienced and female, she had a better diagnostic grasp of goats than any other damn vet in the county—particularly the middle-aged, lab-obsessed males.

"Of course, it could be listeriosis," she mused out loud.

"What's that?" Danto asked, grasping for straws.

"It's also called circling disease. The goats head press first, then start acting funny, and then just begin to circle. It comes from a bacteria in the soil ingested through the goat's mouth or via an eye infection."

"Is it bad?" Danto asked.

"Sometimes . . . but if you catch it early, antibiotics do the trick."

"These goats ain't circling," Charlie said. He always had to put his two cents in, Didi thought. But he was right. And Danto agreed.

Didi squatted on the ground like an Indian, folded her hands pensively in front of her, and watched Laura browse. She blocked out Danto and Charlie and the time and the weather. She studied Laura carefully for about three minutes from her squatting position, then stood and approached the goat.

"What a lovely goat you are, Miss Laura," Didi whispered in a playful manner and slowly began to scratch the top of the doe's head. French Alpine goats are exquisite, Didi mused—perfectly proportioned, a bit haughty, a bit inquisitive.

"Are you going to tell me what's bothering you, Miss Laura, or make me find out for myself?" she cooed into one of Laura's lovely erect ears. All Laura said in response was the same whispery bleat.

Didi kept watching her. It was obvious that Laura was experiencing some kind of discomfort—intermittently. But, Didi reasoned, it could not be pain. She was just too placid between bouts. And goats in pain often vented their aggression against themselves or went into isolation. No, it wasn't pain.

Didi scratched Laura's chest this time, staring into the goat's eyes. "Now, Miss Laura, I don't give a damn if you are the best milking goat in all of Dutchess County. If you don't tell me what's ailing you, I'm going to . . ."

It was decidedly unprofessional behavior from a vet trained at that temple of scientific veterinary medicine, the University of Pennsylvania, but somehow it worked. Didi broke off her sentence halfway through, stared incredulously at her own scratching hand and then let out a whoop that spooked poor Laura.

Turning to Danto, she called out: "Of course! Laura has an itch! She has an itch she can't get to. So she and the other goats slam their heads because it's an itch within. It has to be inside the ears!"

Then Didi turned to Charlie, who was standing with the notebook closed, obviously having once again forgotten to take notes. She ignored his incompetence. "Charlie! Go to the jeep and bring me the microscope. It's buried somewhere in the back, in a wooden case." Charlie gave her an "is this really necessary?" look and then trudged off.

She waited with Danto in silence. She looked much younger than her twenty-eight years—small and thin with short black hair, bangs, and very pale green eyes. "Pretty as a picture" everyone had always said about her. She was wearing overalls with crisscross straps, a Greenpeace Save The Whales sweatshirt with a hood, and a pair of enormous, rubber mud boots with the tops turned down.

Charlie finally returned, puffing and lugging the case. "Do me a favor, Charlie. Set the scope up on the case and take out the slides and the solution."

Didi removed long-stem cotton swabs from her leather satchel and signaled to Danto that he should hold the goat.

She waited until Danto was holding Laura still and then swabbed deep into her left ear.

She walked to the case on which the battered microscope now sat, rolled the swab onto one of the slides, fixed it with a drop of solution, and slid it under the lens.

Didi squatted close to the ground for a full minute, looking into the scope. Then she stood up, grinning, and said to Danto: "Take a look."

The large man had to be helped into a squatting position and supported while he gazed at the slide.

"My God!" he said. "They have legs!"

Didi laughed and helped him up. "Yes," she said, "they sure do. They are mites. Your goats are infected with Psoroptic mange."

Howard Danto's face turned ashen. "That's fatal, isn't it?" he whispered.

Didi shook her head vigorously. "No! No! You're thinking of Sarcoptic mange. That's deadly and ugly. No, this kind of mange can be quickly cleared up with any one of a dozen commercial washes. Just squirt it in the ears using one of those rubber syringes, like people use for ear wax."

Danto heaved a sigh of relief. He wiped his enormous face with a small-checked handkerchief.

Didi looked at her watch. It was ten minutes to eight. Even if she left immediately, she would still be late for the meeting. But, if she drove back to her place, picked up the medication, and brought it back to Danto—she would be very, very late and probably would have to miss the meeting altogether. It was a problem; she wanted very much to help Danto administer the wash the first time.

Her thoughts raced. It wasn't an important meeting. She had been named coordinator of the anti-rabies effort in the area by the director of the County Agricultural Extension Service, mainly because none of the other vets were willing. There wasn't much anyone could do really—the rabies epidemic was now in its fifth year. If the people didn't realize that they had to cover their garbage, report crazed raccoons, and leash their dogs, then no amount of meetings would help. But if she didn't show up, she'd miss talking to Dick Obey, probably her only real friend in the town. He was a wonderful and wise dairy farmer whose operation had gone bust in 1989, whose wife had died of cancer in 1985, and whose son had been killed in Vietnam in 1970. He still clung to his land, doing all sorts of odd jobs. It was Dick Obey who had made sure that farmers in the area used her as a vet when she had first hung out her shingle.

He never admitted to that, but she knew it was true. After the meetings in the diner, Didi and Obey always went into town together and talked about a million things. It was an interlude both always looked forward to . . . it was the real reason they both showed up religiously for the meetings. No, she had to get to the meeting.

"Look, Mr. Danto, I have an appointment at the Hillsbrook Diner that I just can't break. My assistant, Charlie, is going to drop me off there, then pick up the ear wash, and come back here. He'll help you administer it."

"That's fine . . . that's OK," Howard Danto said. "I'm much obliged for what you have done. Obliged and grateful."

"Do you understand, Charlie?" Didi asked. Charlie Gravis nodded his grizzled head.

Danto walked them back to the jeep, reiterating over and over again his gratitude. They shook hands finally and the red jeep moved off.

"Do you understand, Charlie? I'll get out at the Hillsbrook Diner. You take the jeep, go back to the house, get the wash, and deliver it to Danto. Help him with the goats." She handed Charlie a slip of paper with the name of the substance that had to be delivered. "Take a couple of rubber syringes and just show him how to do it."

Charlie seemed to scrunch down in his seat. "You know, Miss Quinn," he said, "a strong hot vinegar wash with a few garlic cloves would do just as well."

"Damn it, Charlie! Follow my instructions!" Didi responded angrily. This was one client that Didi didn't want corrupted by Charlie's herbal wisdom.

"You're the boss," Charlie said.

"I guess I am."

At eight-twenty, the red jeep pulled off the road in front of the Hillsbrook Diner. Didi ran out of the vehicle into the diner, through the front area, and into the back room, which had since time immemorial, been a popular community meeting place.

Several tables had been pushed together. The committee was waiting for her. There was John Theobold, dairy farmer from Long Road; Roger Brice, dairy farmer from Spindle Road, right across from Didi's land; Frank Draper, owner of the most successful organic farm in Dutchess County, whose clients were some of the poshest restaurants in Manhattan; and George Hammond, the county agent.

"It's about time," said Frank Draper. Didi apologized for being late but her eyes were searching for Dick Obey.

He wasn't there. The chair he usually sat dozing in, near the wall, was occupied. But not by Dick Obey. By a New York state trooper in full regalia: wide hat, leather holster and belt, creased uniform, shoulder strap, shining boots.

"Well, damn it, tell her," she heard John Theobold instruct the trooper.

He removed his elegant, wide-brimmed hat and stared at Didi Quinn Nightingale. "Mr. Obey was found this morning. On Route 28, outside Delhi, in Delaware County. He had been drinking heavily and fell onto the side of the road. A pack of stray dogs must have found him there, unconscious. We discovered the body just as it got light. He was dead. His jugular ripped out. The dogs must have gone berserk."

ENTER THE
MYSTERIOUS WORLD OF
ALICE NESTLETON IN
HER LYDIA ADAMSON
SERIES . . . BY READING
THESE OTHER PURR-FECT
CAT CAPERS FROM SIGNET

A CAT IN THE MANGER

Alice Nestleton, an off-off Broadway actress-turned-amateur sleuth, is crazy about cats, particularly her Maine coon, Bushy, and alley cat, Pancho. Alice plans to enjoy a merry little Christmas peacefully cat-sitting at a gorgeous Long Island estate, where she expects to be greeted by eight howling Himalayans. Instead, she stumbles across a grisly corpse. Alice has unwittingly become part of a deadly game of high-stakes horse racing, sinister seduction, and missing money. Alice knows she'll have to count on her catlike instincts and (she hopes!) nine lives to solve the murder mystery.

A CAT OF A DIFFERENT COLOR

Alice Nestleton returns home one evening after teaching her acting class at the New School to find a lovestruck student bearing a curious gift—a beautiful white Abyssinian-like cat. The next day, the student is murdered in a Manhattan bar and the rare cat is cat-napped! Alice's feline curiosity prompts her to investigate. As the clues unfold, Alice is led into an underworld of smuggling, blackmail and murder. Alice sets one of her famous traps to uncover a criminal operation that stretches from downtown Manhattan to South America to the center of New York's diamond district. Alice herself becomes the prey in a cat-and-mouse game before she finds the key to the mystery in a group of unusual cats with an exotic history.

A CAT IN WOLF'S CLOTHING

When two retired city workers are found slain in their apartment, the New York City police discover the same clue that has left them baffled in seventeen murder cases in the last fifteen years—all of the murder victims were cat owners, and a toy was left for each cat at the murder scene. After reaching one too many dead ends, the police decide to consult New York's cagiest crime-solving cat expert, Alice Nestleton. What appears to be the work of one psychotic, cat-loving murderer leads to a tangled web of intrigue as our heroine becomes convinced that the key to the crimes lies in the cats, which mysteriously vanish after the murders. The trail of clues takes Alice from the secretive small towns of the Adirondacks to the eerie caverns beneath Central Park, where she finds that sometimes cat-worship can lead to murder.

A CAT BY ANY OTHER NAME

A hot New York summer has Alice Nestleton taking a hiatus from the stage and joining a coterie of cat-lovers in cultivating a Manhattan herb garden. When one of the cozy group plunges to her death, Alice is stunned and grief-stricken by the apparent suicide of her close friend. But aided by her two cats, she soon smells a rat. And with the help of her own felinelike instincts, Alice unravels the trail of clues and sets a trap that leads her from the Brooklyn Botanical Gardens right to her own backyard. Could the victim's dearest friends have been her own worst enemies?

A CAT IN THE WINGS

Cats, Christmas, and crime converge when Alice Nestleton finds herself on the prowl for the murderer of a once world-famous, ballet dancer. Alice's close friend has been charged with the crime and it is up to Alice to discover the truth. From Manhattan's meanest streets to the elegant salons of wealthy art patrons, Alice is drawn into a dark and dangerous web of deception, until one very special cat brings Alice the clues she needs to track down the murderer of one of the most imaginative men the ballet world has ever known.

A CAT WITH A FIDDLE

Alice Nestleton's latest job requires her to drive a musician's cat up to rural Massachusetts. Hurt by bad reviews of her latest play, Alice looks forward to a long restful weekend. But though the woods are beautiful and relaxing, Alice must share the artists' colony with a world-famous quartet beset by rivalries. Her peaceful vacation is shattered when the handsome lady-killer of a pianist turns up murdered. Alice may have a tin ear, but she has a sharp eye for suspects and a nose for clues. Her investigations lead her from the scenic Berkshire mountains to New York City, but it takes the clue of a rare breed of cat for Alice to piece together the puzzle. Alice has a good idea "whodunit," but the local police won't listen so our intrepid cat-lady is soon baiting a dangerous trap for a killer.

Wouldn't you know that the one thing to come along and ruin a perfect trip would be my crazy cat Pancho.

There I was, seated sumptuously in a *private jet*. On the last leg of a seven-hour flight from New York to Marseilles. I'd never been there before, but I just knew it was going to be singularly . . . atmospheric. And so I sat there luxuriating in the huge leather seat, the engines humming quietly somewhere in the sleek steel bird's belly. By turns, I sipped my chichi mineral water and dozed—my dreams full of muscular little Frenchmen and long-legged ladies *Apache* dancing; miscellaneous scenes from the musical *Fanny*; and the best fish soup in the whole wide world.

But the story gets even better than that. I was on my way to becoming a movie star! I'd actually landed a featured part in a thriller that was being shot in southern France.

Ahead of me, in a black wool Calvin Klein that had set her back four figures, was Dorothy Dodd, who was bankrolling the film. At her right hand was her young lover, Ray Allen Penze, the star of the venture. On the seats across from them were three cat carriers, each holding one of Dorothy's beautiful Abyssinian cats.

In the row behind them, a small mountain of plastic martini glasses on his fold-down tray, was Sidney Rice, the gentle, fine British actor who would play the other male lead.

Then there was ebullient Brian Watts, the producer who had hired me. Accompanying him was Cilla Hood, Brian's recently acquired bedmate, a beautiful, youngish blonde whom he had met only a few months before at a New York party and promised an unforgettable trip to the south of France. Well, he hadn't been far off the mark on that one.

It all seemed impossibly glamorous: an entire, fabulously appointed jet hired just to carry five people and five cats across the Atlantic. As my old friend Anthony Basillio might put it, Dorothy Dodd was no piker.

Wait a minute . . . correction; *six* people. I forgot to include myself in the tally. Me: the female lead, "the woman," the final principal in this three-character epic, *The Emptying*. The whole show would be placed in the hands of Claude Braque, one of the more prestigious second-string European directors.

The money they offered me was incredible—by my standards, anyway. And the last concession they made to me sealed my participation—they said I could bring along my cats. Which brings me back to Pancho.

The first six hours of the flight had been delightfully restful. That quiet time had helped me to recover from the two last insane weeks in New York, during which I had experienced what could only be called a spending frenzy. I'd spent damn near fourteen solid days shopping. The $19,500 advance I received, after agent's commission, had unhinged me. That was more money than I'd ever seen at one time in my life. I wined and dined Basillio royally, I bought gifts for my neighbor, Mrs. Oshrin, and my girlfriends, lavished toy mice and gourmet fish on my cat-sitting charges. And I nearly cleaned out the fancy Madison Avenue pet boutiques with things for my own felines, Bushy and Pancho. As for the things I purchased for myself . . . I'm simply too embarrassed to go over the list. Oh, what a glorious time I was having.

So, even though I usually hate flying, this trip was a day at the beach. And then Pancho struck.

According to the captain—I guess that's what the person ferrying the five of us was called—we were about an hour out of Marseilles. I thought the cats deserved a treat for being so cooperative, sitting patiently in their little mobile prisons. So I retrieved the plastic baggie full of dried liver snaps and opened Bushy's carrier to give him a few. The big Maine coon threw me a martyred look, but he took the snap.

Then I began gingerly to push one in through the grille of Pancho's box. At just that moment he banged his head heavily against the cell door. The clasp popped open and out flew Pancho.

Out flew my half-tailed, battleship gray, paranoid mongrel, starting the lunatic run of his life, leaping from seat to luggage rack and back again, clawing at upholstery and throwing himself against the windows—a one-cat tornado. All accompanied by startled shrieks and curses from the other passengers.

"Pancho!" I screamed as he disappeared up the aisle. *"Please!"*

Silence.

Then the loudspeaker in the cockpit went on

and we heard a booming male voice, full of panic and rage: "Hey! Out there—hey! . . . Someone come and get this damn cat out of here!"

I raced into the pilot's cabin. Pancho was sitting calmly atop the blinking control panel, daintily making his toilette.

The copilot looked blackly at me and began in a low, threatening tone, "If you don't get the—"

I grabbed Pancho by one of his wet paws and made my way swiftly back to my seat. I could hear Dorothy cooing placatingly to her three cats, still in their carriers. Pancho gave me little trouble going back inside his cell. "You little criminal," I whispered, "this is the last time you'll ever leave Twenty-Sixth Street."

Marseilles was cold. But it wasn't like a New York February there. There was moisture in the cool air, a reminder in the wind that the sea was nearby. After a perfunctory inspection at Customs, we were ushered out of a side door at the airport, where two spanking new rented Volkswagen vans waited.

Director Claude Braque was driving one of them. He was a tall, craggy man with healthy-looking, wavy hair; I recognized him immediately, noting that he was wearing the same safari jacket I'd seen in photos of him. The driver of the other vehicle was a young woman. Wearing jeans and a storm coat, she introduced herself as "Alison." Her blond hair was held back with a series of Chinese combs, and she wore a pair of those stylish sunglasses with midnight-black lenses.

The moment they spotted us they stepped out of their respective vans. "*Bienvenue!*" Braque called to us. "Welcome to France."

The young woman produced a bottle with the unmistakable orange Veuve Cliquot label and distributed paper cups all around. Braque expertly maneuvered the cork out of the chilled bottle and we all sipped. I drank mine, cringing at the "Hollywood" spectacle we were making. Clearly we would not be allowed to leave until the bottle was empty. I wondered if someone would be delegated to smash the empty against the fender of the nearest vehicle.

"Ridiculous!" I heard a minute later. I turned to see Brian Watts, who had spoken, a few feet away. *What's ridiculous?* I wondered. *The champagne? The movie we were about to make?* But then I realized he was speaking to Dorothy Dodd, who stood next to her young lover, Ray Allen. A few words I couldn't hear were exchanged between the three of them. And then Ray Allen impulsively took Dorothy in his arms and planted a long, lingering kiss on her mouth. Well, I thought, perhaps some would think that kind of display was ridiculous, but I had done more foolish things than that in the recent past—when I'd had the mixed blessing of being in love with a younger man.

The shouting resumed a minute later. It seemed that Dorothy wanted to drive one of the vans herself, and Brian and Ray Allen were opposed to it. Miss Dodd, however, won the day. She was the boss, after all. She was paying for everything. I watched her climb into the Volkswagen.

Off we went—Dorothy at the wheel in the lead car. Next to her was Ray Allen Penze. Sidney Rice and Claude Braque, who presumably would be directing Dorothy to the village where we were staying, sat in back.

I was in the second van, seated next to Cilla

Hood. Brian took the passenger seat next to the pretty blond production assistant.

Our destination was the small seacoast village of Ste. Ruffin, located in southwestern Provence, in the Camargue. It was a fascinating if little-known part of the country—a large area of grassy plains, salt marshes, and dunes, where the tributaries of the Rhone reach the sea.

We hadn't gone many miles west from Marseilles when our surroundings began to undergo a transformation. Soon we were driving through a terrain that seemed to belong more to some remote archipelago than to Europe. There seemed to be a complete absence of green in the landscape. The winter wind, the legendary *mistral*, blew steadily—not freezing but relentless—though the sun was breaking brilliantly above us.

"Obviously, this is *not* high season in the Camargue," Cilla observed.

I thought she was merely making an observation, but Brian took it as an attack on him. "That's the reason we got the permits to shoot in Ste. Ruffin," he said roughly. "Because the tourist season is spring and fall. The village will be empty now. That's why we were able to rent the whole inn for twenty-one days, for a tenth of the usual nut." He seemed to grow more and more angry. "Besides that, winter light is *unbelievable* here! Arles is only a few miles north. Why do you think Van Gogh went there—for the fish soup?"

The van slowed down precipitously. We were all being jerked about, including my cats, who seemed to have accepted their fate—I didn't hear a peep from them.

"Sorry," Alison said, adjusting her glasses. "The

other van keeps speeding up and then slowing again."

"What the hell is she doing—sightseeing?" Brian said. He peered ahead at the other car. "And what the hell *is* she seeing?" he added, a note of worry in his voice. "She's got the rearview mirror turned down."

"Would you mind closing your window, Brian?" Cilla asked evenly. "I'm getting cold."

He rolled the window up a few inches, but not enough to cure the problem. The wind continued to rake us in back. Brian was a lovely man, but sometimes he could be difficult.

I had been told there were loads of horse farms in the Camargue. In fact, a bawdy acquaintance of mine had told me that a pampas cowboy was probably just what I needed at this time in my life. I was keeping half an eye out, but I didn't see anything that looked like a French wrangler about.

Soon enough, we all tired of the scenery, or the lack thereof. I closed my eyes, but I wasn't sleeping. Just reflecting on the sheer absurdity of it all. About ten hours ago I was in my pajamas, drinking coffee from my favorite cup and looking out my window at the out-of-business housewares store. Now I was in the French countryside thinking about lonesome cowboys. It *did* seem . . . wrong, somehow, that you could get to the other side of the globe in less than half a day.

And something else seemed absurd: how, for all these years, I'd had the temerity to spurn virtually any stage role that did not come up to my bizarre, rarefied standards—yet I leaped at the chance to do what was probably going to be a stinker of a movie. Was it the money? Yes and no. Was it that I felt it was high time for me to be recognized on the street by the general public? Well, yes and no. Was it that I needed to get away from Manhattan? Yes.

"Will it be much longer?" I heard Brian ask our driver.

"No," said Alison. "We're very close now. Soon you'll see a small church with a low wall in front. It comes up suddenly. We just take a sharp left, and in a few minutes we'll be on the main street."

"Where the Ste. Ruffin marching band will play us into town," Cilla quipped mockingly. But Brian was too preoccupied to share the joke.

"Here it comes," said Alison.

I opened my eyes. The squat little church with its white stone wall was gorgeous.

"And here's where we make the turn," the young woman said confidently.

I reached out instinctively to steady the cats in their carriers.

But the van in front of us did not turn left. And it did not slow down at all. It accelerated! And a second later it slammed into the stone wall with sickening force.

The four of us sat in the van for a few awful seconds, not knowing what to do. Then, Brian was jumping from the car and running, yelling back to us as he moved, "Hurry!"

Cilla was the first to obey. She threw open her door and began running toward him, crying all the while.

The front of the van was decimated.

Ray Allen Penze had been thrown from the vehicle and was on all fours on the ground. He was dazed, babbling—"Accidents will happen," was what he was saying, I think. Still, he seemed essentially unhurt.

Sidney Rice had landed between the seats. I could hear him breathing, but he was not moving at all.

Claude was sitting erect on the backseat, looking extremely alert, if haunted. He stared expressionlessly at us through the rear window, shaking his head ever so slightly. Then he sighed once.

Dorothy obviously had not been wearing her seat belt.

She had gone right through the windshield, so that half her body lay on the crumpled hood, the other half snagged grotesquely on the wheel inside.

The jagged windshield had very nearly severed her head. Her lifeless eyes stared straight ahead, past the wall to the old church beyond.

Brian seemed mesmerized by the dangling head. He was pulling me toward it, though I don't know when it was that he'd taken hold of my hand, and I was resisting his tugs.

Finally bursting into action, Alison raced back to our van and roared off toward the village.

"She's going for help," Brian explained needlessly. "I know what happened," he added, sounding feverish.

Cilla and I turned to him.

"*I* know what it was," he went on. "She went for the brake and hit the accelerator instead. She wanted to brake for the turn . . . and instead her . . . her . . . she hit the gas and . . ."

Brian's face was clown white. I thought he might faint. But he didn't. He exploded into tears. "My God! One tiny mistake! One wrong step—just one . . ."

It was then that I remembered Dorothy's animals—the Abyssinians. I rushed around the back of the van and wrested open the hatchback. One of the carriers lay on its side. The others had gone sliding, and now rested at crazy angles to each other. I pulled out all three, set them carefully on the ground and, one by one, cracked open the luxe, velvet-lined cages to look in on the occupants.

I was not personally acquainted with these three beauties, but I knew the meaning of the sounds they were making: feed me—now. I knew that as long as they were hungry, they'd be fine. It was only their mistress—our benefactor, the impeccably dressed, reed thin, outrageously rich, very dead Dorothy Dodd—who would never be hungry again.

About the Author

Lydia Adamson is the pseudonym of a noted mystery writer who lives in New York.